Graeme Gordon lives in London. He has been a struggling actor, a struggling playwright and a struggling film-maker. This is his first novel.

Other Mask Noir Titles

BAYSWATER BODYCOUNT

Graeme Gordon

Special thanks to John & Rikki and Peter & Isabel

Library of Congress Catalog Card Number: 95-68385

A full catalogue record for this book can be obtained from
the British Library on request

The right of Graeme Gordon to be identified as the author of
this work has been asserted by him in accordance with the
Copyright, Designs and Patents Act 1988

'I Will Survive' written by Frederick Perren and Dino Fekaris
© 1978 PolyGram Music Publishing Limited
Lyrics reproduced by kind permission of the publishers

Copyright © 1995 Graeme Gordon

First published in 1995 by Serpent's Tail,
4 Blackstock Mews, London N4, and
180 Varick Street, 10th floor, New York, NY 10014

Set in 10pt ITC Century Book by CentraCet, Cambridge
Printed in Great Britain by Cox & Wyman Ltd., Reading,
Berkshire

for Jo

CHAPTER 1

The Jewish boy was sweating.

Clear drops sprang from the roots of his matted black hair, trickled down each long curl and fell one by one to the cracked stone floor. He swallowed carefully, with difficulty. The longest blade of a lovingly maintained Swiss army knife was pressed tight against his throat by a steady, sandy-brown hand.

The hand belonged to Mo, a thick-set young Arab with a grim, fixed stare. He rocked slowly back and forth on his heels, muttering into David's terrified, purple face.

'What's a filthy, stinking, bastard Jew doing in *my* neighbourhood?'

Mo's friend Tayeb stood leaning against the storeroom door, frankly bored with the whole interrogation routine. More than two hours earlier, he had been happy enough to help tie the Jew's feet together and hang him upside down from a spare meathook between a pair of whole skinned lambs. It had even seemed funny at the time. But now it was nearly four in the morning, he was tired and cold – and nobody was laughing any more.

'C'mon, man,' he yawned, 'I reckon the kid's had enough. Why don't we just dump him back on the street and get the fuck out of here?'

'Not till I get some answers,' Mo insisted.

Tayeb wanted to argue with him, but he couldn't think of anything else to say. And now he needed to take a leak. He wandered over to the furthest, darkest corner of the room and stood facing the wall. Since he felt a little self-conscious, it took him a while to get a decent stream going.

David was all of fifteen years old. He was a studious boy, but none of his classes at school had dealt with the subject of how to behave under torture. The silent approach seemed to be wearing one of the Arabs down – but not the one with the knife.

'Answer me, motherfuck!'

There was a new edge to Mo's voice. Anger and impatience made him even more dangerous. David knew he had to say something – anything to appease the Arab monster. He tried to clear his throat. A gobbet of phlegm plastered itself over his airway, nearly choking him. He swallowed, spluttered and spat – right into Mo's threatening face.

Mo scarcely seemed to react. He just blinked. David watched the spit running down his face, watched the corners of Mo's mouth twitch ever so slightly upwards.

'I – I didn't mean to . . .' he stammered.

Smiling broadly now, Mo drew the fine steel blade swiftly across the boy's neck, cutting deep down to the bone. David's head flapped back, sending a shower of sweat flying towards the floor and exposing a half-inch layer of veiny white fat over a dark red, empty slit. The sweat hit the floor as the blood started to flow.

Tayeb shook off his dick, put it away, zipped up and turned around.

'What the fuck . . .?!' he shouted.

The Jewish boy's body convulsed spasmodically, his heart heaving thick spurts of blood out through the gaping wound. Some of it ran down a ceramic gutter into a drain. Most of it sprayed across the floor and up the walls. The rest of it showered over the two young Arabs.

'Shit!'

They both moved at once, making for the door which said EMERGENCY EXIT. This was an emergency. They didn't stop to read the other sign which said WARNING! THIS DOOR IS ALARMED.

Tayeb hit the bar with his full nine-and-a-half-stone weight and the door swung open. Mo checked his pace too late. They landed in a tangle of limbs on top of a heap of rotting plastic bin bags. The alarm started ringing as the two youths shook themselves apart, then ran skidding and stumbling out into the street and away.

The building which they had just broken out of belonged to a small grocery chain called the High Street Cash and Carry Emporium. A handwritten sign in the window assured its customers they were getting the best fresh halal meat daily.

The early morning sun rose over the wrought-iron gazebo at the bottom of Mrs Dexter's garden. The lady of the house was stretched out on a lounger in the conservatory, fast asleep. Her skin looked grey, even through the solarium tan, and she had a trace of a moustache – though, generally speaking, the electrolysis sessions had been a great success. Tiny beads of perspiration picked out the few wispy hairs that had got away.

The doorbell chimed – and Mrs Dexter was awake. She sat up and rubbed her eyes until they were quite red and weepy. Then she shuffled off along the hall to the front door, scattering a pile of women's magazines in her wake. A trial tampon for medium to heavy flow fell out of one of them, but she was too upset to notice.

She opened her mouth at the same time as the door, but no sound came out. It wasn't David. It was a nervous little boy in a policeman's uniform. The boy was telling her that David was dead. She started explaining to him that David hadn't come home yet, so he couldn't possibly . . .

Her legs gave way and she sat down with a dull thud. The policeman tried to think of something helpful to say but his head was filled with the one thought that fat people don't bounce – they spread. He readjusted his helmet to kill some time. He had nothing to do. She hadn't fainted, she'd just sat down, so he couldn't put her into the recovery position or radio for assistance, or anything.

Then she started to scream.

At the other end of the road the milkman did a one-point turn in his float, heading away from the sound before he realised what he was doing. He ploughed straight into the side of a special edition Mercedes sports which was backing out of a private garage. The two drivers were out of their seats and hurling recriminations at one another before the last carton of orange juice had burst on the ground.

A pair of sharply dressed midgets, on their way home from an all-night poker game around the corner, sidled up on the blind side of the badly damaged float and lifted a packet of bacon, a white sliced loaf and a pint of milk – then did a fast fade.

The head neighbourhood-watch curtain twitcher dashed out from her porch to stake her claim as a witness, tripped over the early edition of the *Daily Mail* and buried her face in the crazy paving, fracturing a cheekbone.

The policeman breathed a deep sigh of relief and radioed for assistance.

'It's too bad that Rabin and Jerry ran out of money,' said Emmy, with not a hint of sincerity.

'I'll have you next,' grunted Isaac, a malproportioned, muscular dwarf.

'I think not. I'm folding.'

Emmy stacked his five cards neatly face downwards and leaned back in his chair.

'Gutless shit.'

'If you say so.'

Isaac looked up, checking out the other players. There were only four left at the table, which meant that this hand was down to him, Leon and Josh.

The room was about one third lit by a single, shaded bulb hanging over the poker table. All natural light was rigorously excluded by stainless steel, continental-style, roll shutters. Nobody present was over four feet three inches in height: it was a house rule.

As Isaac pondered the betting, his shirt tail flopped over the back of his stool and trailed across the remains of a 9-Spice takeout which he had dumped behind him more than six hours earlier.

'Slam!'

Leon, the midget immediately to Isaac's left, passed him a litre bottle of tequila from the centre of the table. He gulped about half an inch, held it in the back of his throat, and brought his meaty forehead down smack on the table in front of him. After a moment's immobility, he swallowed and let out a short, rasping burst of laughter. Baby-faced Leon giggled nervously; the dwarf was that far out of his tree, he could do anything. Except stand up.

Isaac stuck a crumpled fiver in the pint glass they used for the pot.

'Raise you – bastards,' he growled.

Leon took his time deciding whether to raise or fold on a pair of weak threes. His speciality was the double bluff.

He worked hard at making the slight hesitations that would suggest he held a very strong hand, but was trying to disguise the fact. Eventually, he raised.

Rachel, Leon's wife and business partner, sat in the darkest corner of the room, her face illuminated by the flame of a tiny gas camp stove. Her pupils were so dilated there was no way of telling what colour her eyes might be.

Two cheap dinner knives were jammed under the grid of the stove, the blades glowing red. Rachel leaned carefully over to one side and picked up a large plastic lemonade bottle between her teeth. The bottle was empty – she had cut off the bottom end with a bread knife at the start of the evening.

Panting weakly through the bottle-neck, she extracted one of the knives and dabbed up a lump of dark brown resin on its tip. The hash steamed gently. She took as deep a breath as her aching lungs would allow, held the first knife under the end of the bottle and pressed the second knife firmly against it.

Dense clouds of white smoke billowed up towards her mouth, which she sucked in vigorously. She held it down for as long as she could, finally breathing out the thin, grey exhaust which her body had failed to absorb. Completely wrecked at last, she collapsed gratefully into swirling, empty inner space.

The betting had gone two more rounds and Josh had joined Emmy in dropping out of the hand. Leon's arteries were running sour with adrenalin. He no longer knew what cards he held – it made no difference – all he had to do was outbet the dwarf.

He threw two weeks' rent money into the middle of the table and waited, absolutely motionless. Isaac glanced up at him, his hand starting towards his cards, intending to push them away in disgust. As he did so, an almost imperceptible movement by Leon – perhaps of his head settling back down on the end of his neck – made Isaac think better of folding. Instead, he met Leon's bet with an evil grin.

'See you.'

Leon wasn't ready for this. He was sure Isaac had been bluffing with, at the very best, as crap a hand as his own. He started to feel sick. He had lost his nerve, and the dwarf was waiting to collect.

The telephone rang, and the fine wire of tension connecting the two men suddenly snapped. Leon jumped up the back of his chair, slumped forward and threw up over the table. Isaac fell off his stool, then lumbered across the room to answer the phone. Emmy and Josh pushed themselves back in their chairs, out of range of the spreading pool of vomit. It dripped steadily on to the nylon carpet, mixing in with the fag ash and nail clippings that had always been there.

Isaac kicked the receiver off the hook and managed to snatch it up at his third attempt. He started to swear incoherently into the mouthpiece but suddenly sobered when he recognised the voice at the other end of the line.

'Come to work, Zak.'

Having issued this order, Steven Louis Dexter, father to the late David Dexter and chairman of the North London Property Holding Corporation, hung up. He walked back into the conservatory, kissed his wife on the forehead and went out, leaving her heavily sedated body in the professionally comforting arms of the Medicare nurse.

CHAPTER 2

'Fucking no-legs wanker,' groaned Rabin, when he played back the message Isaac had left on their answerphone.

Jerry put the bacon under the grill and came out of the closet-sized kitchen into the bedsit room.

The room was only just big enough to accommodate their double mattress, let alone anything else – but it *was* cheap. Its one window was well below street level, which would have given the place a dirty, dingy feel even if the window hadn't been caked with filth.

Jerry kissed Rabin on the tip of his nose.

'Yeah, I know – but we could really use the dosh.'

'I'm not getting at you – it's him, ordering us about cos he knows we need the fucking money – '

'Forget it,' said Jerry. 'We can't do anything for hours yet, anyway.'

He gave Rabin a quick hug and went back into the kitchen. Rabin followed him through and spread a couple of slices of bread with the last scrapings of marge. A tin pan of water started to boil on top of the two-ring stove. The other ring had packed in years ago.

'D'you want to make the tea?' asked Jerry.

Rabin reached for the pan, burned himself on the hot metal, swore violently, then wrapped a cloth round his hand and poured the water. Both mugs were brown, chipped and not terribly clean. Neither handle had survived Rabin's infrequent attempts at washing up.

Like the other midgets, Jerry and Rabin were gentiles.

They had all taken mock-Jewish pseudonyms when they started working for what they called the Kosher Klan. The rest of the time the two of them worked as novelty rent boys, either individually or together – if the money was good. Which it usually was. Demand was limited, however.

Where possible, they booked appointments by phone, which was safer than working the streets. But if the regulars weren't calling up, they had to go out and pull. When they were really broke, Rabin would take S/M work – which usually meant dressing up as a schoolboy and letting some middle-aged family man take out life's little frustrations on his backside with a sex shop cane.

Tonight they would be trawling for information, so they were going to have to be very choosy about who they went with – though not in the way they normally liked to be.

Jerry watched happily as Rabin took a big, hungry bite of his bacon sandwich. Rabin had once said to him, *We've gotta love each other, baby – no big motherfucker's ever gonna do it.* Jerry had lost count of the number of tricks he had turned long before he ever met Rabin, so he knew that this was the truth.

They finished eating, clinked their ugly brown mugs together and kissed. Jerry found a clean cigarette paper tucked down the side of the mattress. He started rooting through the overflowing ashtray, digging out the longer stubs. Rabin grimaced, then helped him shake the unused ends of tobacco out on to the paper.

Isaac was already at work. Dexter had managed to fiddle him an NUJ card, so he could pose as a freelance journalist and generally stick his nose into police business without arousing too much suspicion.

'Watch out, here comes The Freak Show,' the desk sergeant whispered to a colleague as Isaac hurried into Paddington Green police station.

'Now then, Mr Hamilton,' the sergeant continued, referring to the name on Isaac's badge, 'what can I do you for? We've got blackmail, fraud and robbery fresh in – '

'Sergeant, you really must stop doing that.'

'Doing what?'

'Selling yourself short.'

'I think you must know something I don't,' grinned the policeman.

He enjoyed these games. They provided him with what had become a very rare pleasure during the past few years spent behind that godforsaken desk – an opportunity to show off the wealth of native wit which he had amassed in his time on the beat.

'It must have been idle gossip, then,' said Isaac, a comically disappointed expression spreading across his face. 'Violent murder in back room of Paddington food store . . .'

He paused for effect, watching for the sergeant's reaction. The sergeant, in his effort to hold a poker face, amply revealed the truth of Isaac's assertion.

'Well,' he said carefully, 'if we were holding a suspect then, of course, I'd know all about it. But I don't.'

'In that case, you wouldn't even know who you were looking for, I don't suppose . . .'

Isaac let his voice trail off teasingly.

'Let's just say I wouldn't want to say anything that might upset our good relations with the local *Arabic* community,' stressed the policeman, with what he imagined was reasonable subtlety.

'Oh no, indeed!' laughed the dwarf, throwing up his hands in mock horror. 'It's always the question of the exact identity of the criminal that's such a problem,' he continued meaningfully. 'Don't you agree?'

'You're not wrong,' the sergeant replied, looking back down at his desk and filling out a custody report.

Isaac realised that the interview was over and took his leave as swiftly as possible. He put a bit of distance between himself and the station, then went to find a call box to inform Dexter that his suspicions had been correct. As he stretched up to pull the receiver off the hook, he glanced around at the colourful cards in the booth. The one nearest the bottom, at about eye-level for him, read SMALL 'N' SWEET – UNHURRIED SESSIONS WITH MIDGET MALE MODEL – ALL SERVICES. He smiled, recognising Rabin and Jerry's phone number, stuck his ten pence in the slot and dialled Dexter's office.

Dexter's secretary was used to a lot of shorthand, a little typing and saying, *I am afraid Mr Dexter is not available; how can I help you*? She was not accustomed to using the expression *putting you straight through* and – though in every other respect the perfect PA – she fumbled these words when Mr Hamilton's call arrived.

Dexter was using the hands-free facility on his phone, which allowed him to hold his cup of coffee by the saucer, dunk a shortbread finger in it and speak, all at the same time. What he didn't know was that it made his voice sound weak and tinny at the other end of the line.

'Hello Zak. Make your report.'

Isaac figured that he must have been connected to some sort of sophisticated answering machine, so he waited for the tone.

'Isaac?'

'Mr Dexter?'

'I said, make your report.'

Dexter's voice was tight with irritation. Isaac took a deep breath and dammed up the torrent of obscenities which had gathered just behind his front teeth.

'Must be a bad line. Yeah, you were right about the, er, origins of the, er, parties in question.'

'You sound like a dull American movie, Isaac. What else?'

'That's about it for the moment.'

'Go back to work.'

He leaned forward and flicked a switch on the console, cutting the connection. The shortbread had started to dissolve into his coffee. He placed the cup at arm's length on his desk and buzzed his secretary.

'Yes, Mr Dexter?'

'Will you come through, Miss Holmes?'

She stood up at once, tugged at her pencil skirt to get the creases out of it, and checked her reflection in the small mirror in the top drawer of her filing cabinet – filed under D for Dinner Dates. Pausing only to pick up her shorthand pad and gold-plated fountain pen, she knocked firmly on Dexter's office door and went straight on in: being his PA gave her certain privileges.

A less well disciplined set of stilettos could easily have foundered somewhere along the dozen or so yards of deep-pile carpet on the way to Dexter's desk, but not a pair under Miss Holmes's command. She sat down on the very edge of the chair opposite him, leaning slightly forward, her whole being awaiting his instructions with the same patient devotion that a Mayfair prostitute displays towards a wealthy but impotent client. Dexter unlocked the bottom drawer of his desk, took out a short list of names and telephone numbers and handed it to her.

'I would like you to call every person on this list and give them a message from me . . .'

Miss Holmes examined the list quizzically – she had never seen Dexter's handwriting before, only his signature.

'Tell them that the usual quarterly meeting is to be brought forward to tonight, owing to extraordinary circumstances. If they have other engagements, I strongly advise them to cancel and attend this meeting. Do you understand?'

Miss Holmes nodded her head.

'The numbers you have are all private lines so you shouldn't have any difficulty getting through. If there is a problem, refer that person directly to me. That is all.'

'Yes, Mr Dexter,' she confirmed, rising gracefully from her seat.

'Oh, and get me another coffee would you, Miss Holmes?'

'Yes, Mr Dexter.'

She had said just six words or, to be more exact, three words twice and he was already sick of the sound of her voice. But she was a good PA and there were now very few of those on the market – who didn't see themselves as some kind of trainee manager, that was. He would have to get her to make the catering arrangements as well. He wondered whether his usual organisers would be prepared to take it on at such short notice. *Of course they will*, he thought acidly, *they'll just charge me double for it*.

Stacked against the wall to the right of his desk were six television screens, displaying the latest financial indicators from London, New York and Tokyo. He glanced across at them from time to time, but he felt no urge to play the investment game today. He was grieving the loss of his son in the only way he knew how: by coolly seeking out his murderers and wreaking vengeance on them and their houses.

Dexter scratched his stubbly chin. He would shave only when justice had been done. Let others take it as a sign of mourning, for him it would be a constant, nagging spur to execute his intentions.

CHAPTER 3

Blaring out a pre-recorded trumpet fanfare, The Mobility Church of the Twelve Apostles turned right off the Bayswater Road and ground into Queensway, finally shuddering to a halt by the entrance to the ice rink. Late-night shoppers and skaters fled as the self-styled Apostolians emerged from the decommissioned double-decker bus that was their temple, meeting room and bookshop. The church was painted a friendly pastel pink and featured a life-size frieze of smiling children skipping along its sides to the open platform at the back.

The Apostolians, six clean-cut young white men in suits and ties, converged on a scruffily dressed old woman hunched twitching over a Europa carrier bag: an ageing sinner wrestling with the Devil. In fact, it was Mad Betty wrestling with the top of a half-bottle of Scotch. They stood in a circle around her, held hands and meditated profoundly.

However, the bottle top was highly resistant to prayer power and Betty soon began to tire of their divine intervention. She twisted her head up from its customary position some three inches below her shoulders, cleared her throat noisily and spat down her unintentionally plunging neckline.

'Fark off, why duntcha fark off, farkin' child-proof an' all, won't tell me abaht it, you ain't nah daughter of mine gel, f-f-fark off . . .'

Towards the end of this challenging discourse, viscous

yellow-white fluid started to run from her nose and a withered breast flopped out of her blouse. The Apostolians moved briskly away, each of them having miraculously come to an identical conclusion – that she wasn't really worth saving.

A synthesised jingle, loosely based on the introduction to *O Come All Ye Faithful*, whined out of the church's ageing loudspeaker system.

'Jesus extends a warm welcome to one and all,' the crackly voiceover announced. 'Hear your minister's sermon and *you* shall be saved.'

A renewed flourish from the electronic church organ was followed by a loud metallic chink, then a steady hiss of static. Finally came the deep, echoing voice of the preacher, who remained hidden in the discreetly veiled Holy of Holies at the front of the top deck.

'Our merciful Lord Jesus Christ . . .'

'Hear our prayer,' responded the Apostolians.

'We pray that sinners everywhere may repent and be saved . . .'

'Hear our prayer.'

'We pray for those that are too weak to put away earthly things and seek everlasting life . . .'

'Hear our prayer.'

'We pray for the lost souls that follow false gods . . .'

'Hear our prayer.'

'And we pray most of all for the damned souls that follow false prophets – like *Mohammed*!'

The minister put a special stress on this last prayer. His disciples went wild. Screaming ecstatically in a display of ardent faith, they ran to the back of the bus and hauled out an acoustic guitar and five tambourines.

Inside the bus, Josh put his microphone back on its rest and lit a pre-rolled spliff. Josh and Emmy were co-directors of the church: Josh rustled up the sermons while Emmy cooked the books. It was Dexter's way of insulting and intimidating the predominantly Moslem Arab community without denigrating his own faith. And his lawyers had seen to it that the church was an absolutely legitimate, fully registered charity.

'OK, militant monkeys,' Josh said quietly to himself, 'come and get us.' The church had proved invaluable in the past as an instrument for flushing out hot-headed fanatics, who could then be identified and eliminated at a later, less public moment.

Standing on tiptoe, Josh lifted one corner of the curtain in front of him and peered down at the Apostolians performing below. So far no one had taken the bait. *Which is a bit of a pity*, he thought, *since I'd love to see the pissy-pants pretty-boys getting a smacking*.

He settled back down in his seat, scratched his balls and waited to see if the Lord would hear his prayer.

Leon and Rachel were making their final preparations before going on stage at Trix, a campy, glamour nightspot just off Lexington Street in deepest Soho.

To gain entry to the club, the fun-loving punter follows a series of pink, neon arrows to the end of a dark back alley, following also the smell of piss, puke, sweat and come. In one corner is an unmarked door with neither handle nor lock and, above it, a red light and security camera. If the prospective customer appears sufficiently wealthy and corruptible, the door swings open in silent welcome. Once inside, the transsexual host/ess relieves him of ten pounds in cash and his coat. *Think of this coat as your inhibitions*, s/he simpers. *You can pick them up again on your way out. Now have a ball!*

Changing rooms have been provided by a thoughtful

management for those who wish to recreate a persona that they don't want to live on the streets, whether it's Rubberman, Saviour of the Universe or just The Girl Next Door. And you can check your suit, shirt and tie at the desk, along with the rest of your inhibitions.

Leon and Rachel did three sets a night as the club's main cabaret attraction, The World Famous Miniature Strippers. It was almost time for their nine p.m. early performance. First Rachel, then Leon inhaled deeply over a bottle of poppers. Leon lay down on the floor to enjoy the artificial adrenalin rush, while Rachel went back for another snort.

'I can't seem to get it together tonight,' she moaned.

There was a knock at the door and Trixiebelle D'Amour squeezed into the dressing room. She wore a full-length diamante ballgown and a fake silver fox fur, the two items showing off her aubergine skin and flame-red hair to maximum effect. She clicked her tongue disapprovingly at what she saw.

'Five minutes, darlings,' she rasped, 'and you're going to need every last one of them.'

She turned on her heel – which was quite a feat given her sixteen-stone build and four-inch spikes – and left them to get on with it.

Every week at Trix, the various acts adopted a different theme. This week was Japanese week, reflecting the recent growth in that audience sector. Leon and Rachel had had to spend hours with a kind of sticky paste designed for an instant facelift effect in an effort to make their features more oriental. The twist to their act was that Rachel was dressed as a traditional Japanese page-boy, while Leon was wearing an elaborate geisha girl outfit. The electric bell buzzed the one minute call and they took their place in the wings.

Out on the floor, the failed models and actresses who brought the customers their designer cocktails had been working the atmosphere well. The audience was beginning to buzz with anticipation.

The Queensway crowd was buzzing too – with irritation. The Apostolians were now into their third number and showed no signs of letting up.

Not far from where the church was parked, at a table in front of the Cafe Cappuccino, sat Pappy, an enormous, tousle-haired Greek Cypriot in his early fifties. He was general manager of the local all-night store, and probably the only person in the area who could handle the job. The drunks, dope-heads and small-time crooks who made up the bulk of the clientele all had to be kept in line somehow. Pappy was built like a sumo wrestler and bore the proud reputation of always responding with extreme violence to the slightest provocation.

Next to the cafe, leaning against the glass front of a record shop, were Mo and Tayeb, hanging out. Mo had a vein running down the side of his temple which swelled up whenever he got angry. Right now it looked fit to burst.

'You wanna kick ass, yeah?' guessed Tayeb.

'And then some,' Mo nodded, flicking the lid of his Zippo lighter open and shut.

'Boys . . .'

Tayeb turned to see Pappy grinning at them.

'You've gotta watch yourselves there, boys.'

'Man, you're just too old to see when something needs doing,' Mo said bluntly.

'And I got to be this old by being careful, you get it?'

'Sure,' said Mo. 'But we've been bad all our short lives so we've *had* to be careful.'

'It's your heads,' shrugged Pappy. 'I've been deaf, dumb and blind ever since I came to this stinking grey town.'

Mo stared deep into Pappy's eyes, sussing him out. A moment later he smiled and held up his right hand. They high-fived over the cafe table.

'Just don't come causing any trouble in *my* place,' Pappy warned him.

Mo pulled a face of pure innocence and strode off in the direction of the Apostolians. Tayeb had to break into a jog to catch up with him.

'He could be right, man.'

'You chickening out already?'

'Nah, it's just – well for starters there's six of them and only two of us – '

'Chicken,' hissed Mo.

Tayeb jumped in front of him, forcing him to stop.

'Maybe you've forgotten what you did last night – '

'That hymie fuck?' Mo retorted. 'He fucking gobbed on me, man, it was pure reflex – I've told you a thousand times already – '

'OK, OK – but that ain't gonna bring the kid back, is it?'

'Yeah – you're right,' Mo admitted.

'I know I am,' said Tayeb. 'Anyhow – the last thing we need at this precise moment in time is to go drawing attention to ourselves.'

'You're right there too,' Mo agreed, walking around him. 'That's why we've got a plan.'

'What plan?' asked Tayeb, struggling to keep up.

Onstage at Trix, Leon and Rachel had finished their opening dance routine and started to strip. Leon turned his back to the audience and let the shiny Dralon kimono slide off his body, revealing a studded leather bodice, black stockings and suspenders. Rachel pulled off her jacket and paced sternly around him in tight satin breeches and a baggy silk shirt. It was heavy going. The tinkling Japanese music gave them nothing to work with, and the early evening crowd just sat there, silent and open-mouthed.

Perched on a tall stool at the bar, Trixiebelle sensed what the problem was. She reached behind the counter, pulled out a microphone and started clapping a rhythm into it. Once the beat was established, she backed it up with some distinctly sexual panting sounds and long drawn-out whimpers of excitement as each new piece of clothing was discarded.

The effect on the punters was electric: they started to clap along in time with her and the more extrovert began cheering and whistling as Rachel unlaced Leon's bodice and flung it to the floor. Leon folded his arms over his imaginary breasts as he turned to face the crowd, while Rachel stripped off her shorts to reveal a cunningly padded posing pouch.

'Get 'em off! Get 'em off!' Trixiebelle shouted along to the rhythm she had set up.

The audience enthusiastically took up the chant. Rachel unclipped one of Leon's stockings from his suspender belt and slowly rolled it down.

The Apostolians' performance was provoking a remarkably similar response from their distinctly less enthusiastic audience.

'Get 'em off!'

'Fark off!' echoed Mad Betty, who was clearly beyond redemption.

Someone (as the police later discovered, nobody saw *who*) shoved somebody at the back of the crowd, who bumped into the person in front of him, who leaned heavily on the person in front of her, who lost his footing and fell against one of the Apostolians, knocking him over and smashing his tambourine. A minor scuffle broke out, in the course of which the disciple on the ground was accidentally kicked a number of times and punched in the face once.

While attention was focused on this compelling diversion, Mo led Tayeb up between the edge of the crowd and the side of the bus. He got Tayeb to unscrew the petrol cap while he soaked his handkerchief with lighter fluid. Then he stuffed it in the opening of the fuel tank.

Mo flicked his lighter; the handkerchief flared. The two youths ran to the end of the street and jumped on a number 12 bus for the West End.

Leon had only his lace-trimmed French knickers to go. Rachel stood hidden behind him, pulling off her shirt. Then she grabbed his knickers and whipped them down, revealing his unexpected manhood. Her hands flew to her face in mock astonishment as she stepped out of his shadow. Leon turned and tugged off her pouch as she dropped her arms to display her womanly breasts.

The audience gasped in surprise then roared its approval as Leon and Rachel gathered up their clothes and trooped off back to the dressing room. Trixiebelle smiled contentedly to herself, shouted to the bartender for another daiquiri, and picked up the microphone to announce the next act.

Mo and Tayeb were almost at Lancaster Gate when they heard the explosion. They were alone on the top deck and went crazy: shouting, stamping and punching the air. The old, white conductor started up the stairs to give them a piece of his mind. He was going to check those darkies' passes *really* carefully.

Most of the back third of the Mobility Church of the Twelve Apostles landed in Kensington Gardens, but it shed a trail of used parts as it crossed the Bayswater Road, bringing traffic to a screeching halt. The middle third only made it as far as the entrance to Queensway tube station. The front of the bus smouldered gently at first, then went up in a cloud of flames as the fire reached the carburettor.

The windows of the bus had blown out over the flattened crowd below, along with the windows of adjacent shops and restaurants. People living nearby rushed out to gawp at the chaotic scene, but none of them showed any interest in trying to help the injured. A young couple accepted the invitation of a broken shop window to acquire the microwave of their dreams as a free gift.

Pappy brought his head out from under the cafe table and cautiously opened his eyes. He shook the broken shards of glass off his back and watched the pale, shaken Apostolians pick themselves up off the pavement. Their cut, bruised and angry former audience were starting to get up as well and were looking around for someone to blame. Just as another, more serious scuffle was about to break out, the emergency services arrived on the scene.

Pappy roared with laughter; he laughed until his eyes were brimful with tears and his aching lungs gasped for breath. Still chuckling to himself, he put two pound coins on the table to pay for the coffee, with some over for the entertainment. Then he stood up and wandered away. Being deaf, dumb and blind, Pappy figured that he couldn't have anything useful to tell the police.

CHAPTER 4

Mo and Tayeb jumped off the back of the bus as it turned down Haymarket and made for the nearest Leicester Square cinema. For a fiver each, they bought seats for a limp romantic comedy – and an alibi.

Steven Dexter stood at one end of a vast oval table in the secure back boardroom of a custom-built conference centre in neutral Docklands. Facing him was his opposite number in the competitive world of unscrupulous property dealing: Mohammed Aziz, senior managing partner of the West London Development Partnership. Each of the two principals was flanked by four of his closest associates.

Dexter completed his statement regarding the one item on the evening's agenda: the untimely demise of Mr Dexter junior. Aziz stared out of the window at the lights on the other side of the Thames. He casually gathered a fold in his long, white robes and crossed his legs.

'A regrettable incident but,' he gestured vaguely, 'I fail to see that it concerns us here. We are businessmen.'

He smiled cheerlessly. Dexter scowled back at him.

'This terrorist act was perpetrated in a location owned and controlled by members of your organisation. We also understand that the terrorists are members of *your* community.'

'I hope you are not suggesting – '

'I am relating known facts. I am asking you to put your house in order. I am telling you that our continued cooperation depends upon the suppression of terrorist elements operating within your territory.'

'We own property, we do not own people.'

'Security is very expensive, anticipatory defence even more so. I have no desire to return to paying for them.'

Aziz considered the implications of this last remark. He consulted his colleagues quietly in Arabic. Dexter swore under his breath in Yiddish.

All ten men were old enough to remember the pseudo-religious, paramilitary war that had characterised the early property gains on both sides: repeated arson attacks, quiet assassinations of high-level personnel and continuous harassment of vulnerable tenants.

Through their regular conferences, the two sides had succeeded in establishing certain principles, limiting combat to the marketplace and acts of bad faith to those permissible within *normal business practice*. The peaceful ideals of rumour mongering, predatory takeover bids, racist propaganda and manipulation of council officials had replaced the private armies of the violent past.

'Very well,' Aziz announced. 'We too consider open conflict to be counter-productive and wish to remain within the terms of the General Accord. This affair is not of our making and we refuse to be held responsible but, in the name of good relations, we will support the elimination of the undesirables. However, I must urge caution – for an unjust attack on our people is not justice for yours and reprisals would be certain to follow.'

'We are in essential agreement, then,' Dexter concluded.

He opened the door behind him and signalled to a fresh-faced young man in a navy blue suit, whose lapel badge identified him as Jim Crane, Centre Organiser. Dexter turned back to face the conference.

'I hope that you will all stay to enjoy the entertainments which have been prepared for you. I regret that it would be inappropriate for me to do so. Goodnight, gentlemen.'

Shortly after Dexter's withdrawal, Jim Crane returned to usher the executives into their banqueting suite. The room was furnished according to modern international hotel tastes, but an imaginative design consultant had somehow avoided the feel of an airport departure lounge. To either side of the double doors were buffet tables draped in white linen tablecloths, bearing a selection of artistically presented dishes: halal to the left, kosher to the right.

Behind each table stood three immaculately turned out waiters. All six were of the same height, build and spotless complexion. A string quartet played softly in the corner next to the bar, which boasted the widest range of non-alcoholic beverages and Israeli wine of any licensed premises in London.

The members of the two factions mixed freely, each side hoping to extract useful pieces of information about the other's operations while dropping false clues concerning their own. It was an old game, too well played, and they tired of it by the time they had finished eating.

Dexter's deputy signalled Crane, who had remained standing at the entrance to the suite. Under his direction, the waiters cleared the tables and retired, followed by the barman and musicians. He glanced around the room to make sure everything was in order and, satisfied that it was, departed, closing the doors behind him.

Unattended now, the executives made their way to the far end of the room and took up positions at the edge of a pitch-black hole in the floor, leaning on the brass guard rail which surrounded it. Gradually, the main lights in the room dimmed to a dull, background glow. An overhead spotlight snapped on, revealing a twelve-feet-deep stainless steel pit.

Suddenly, a fully grown male pig lumbered out through a sliding door at the bottom of the pit, squealing and grunting with rage. The boar was received with generous laughter and applause, but this did little to improve its temper. It clumped sullenly round its new pen, snorting at its curved reflection.

The deputy chairman, as acting host, was called upon to open the game. He pulled aside a drape to reveal a rack holding a dozen long, metal poles with pointed ends. Having selected a suitable implement, he returned to the edge of the pit and jabbed it firmly into the pig's rump. The pig squealed piercingly and completed a swift lap of its enclosure to a second burst of appreciative laughter.

According to the rules of etiquette, the game was now open. Each man eagerly grabbed a pole and stuck it in the dancing pig whenever it fell within striking distance.

After just five minutes the pig, running with blood and sweat, had had enough. It stood despondently in the middle of the pit, flinching rather than dancing when prodded. The executives put down their poles and watched as another door slid open. The pig made it halfway to the door then skidded to a halt and jumped back. A pair of pit bull terriers bounded out into the arena.

'One . . . Two . . .' chanted the spectators, as the dogs set about the pig.

By the time they reached seven, there was no pig any more, just chunks of raw, bloody pork. The audience applauded heartily as the spotlight dimmed over the pit and the house lights faded back up.

The house lights were going up in cinema three as well.

'Bullshit – that never happened to no one *never*,' said Tayeb.

'That's the whole point, innit – white trash for white trash,' Mo explained.

They unhooked their legs from the seats in front and shuffled along to the end of the row. Tayeb kicked a giant tub of uneaten popcorn out of his way. A thousand little lumps of caramelised air tumbled down the aisle.

'Oi! Whatcha think you're doing?' shouted the exasperated young usher.

'Sorry, man,' said Tayeb.

'I have to clean that up, you know.'

'OK. I'm sorry.'

'There's another show in ten minutes.'

'So clean the motherfucking shit up, you white motherfucker,' Mo muttered.

'You what?'

'Forget it,' said Tayeb.

They had kept moving and were out of the cinema before the usher could come up with another line. They went and leaned against the park railings in the middle of Leicester Square, wondering what to do next.

'We could go to a club,' Tayeb suggested.

'Yeah? Like where?'

Tayeb looked older than his seventeen years but they could still have major difficulty getting in a lot of places. He thought about it.

'How about Changes?'

'Nah, that's for faggots, man.'

'It ain't – it's mixed,' said Tayeb. 'Who gives a shit,

anyhow? You don't have to *sleep* with nobody you don't want to.'

'OK, let's do it,' Mo agreed finally.

They walked up across Chinatown towards the junction of Oxford Street and Tottenham Court Road, where they would be able to get a bus into Islington.

'Chinatown? More like Chinastreet,' grinned Tayeb.

'At least they've got a street,' said Mo.

Tayeb stopped grinning and glanced across at him. Mo just kept on staring straight ahead, looking out at some horizon which nobody else could see. Certainly not Tayeb, who pulled his baseball cap down over his eyes, trying to look as tough and stylish as he could.

Mo's mind was on The Apocalypse – The Third World War – the war in which the coloured peoples of the world would rise up and unite to destroy the old, white oppressor. He had been expelled from one school for handing in a political history essay entitled 'The Motherfucker of Parliaments' – which was when he first became aware of the white man's fear of criticism. And it was his knowledge of this fear that made him strong.

They reached the bus stop. Mo cuffed Tayeb round the back of his head, making him jump.

'Loosen up, man,' Mo laughed, 'we're meant to be having a good time, remember?'

Tayeb smiled back; they touched fists. It was three quarters to midnight and they were just warming up to a wild night out.

CHAPTER 5

Changes is a mixed club in the widest possible sense of the word: mixed race, mixed sex, mixed sexuality, a mixture of quiet secluded booths at the back, loud sound system at the front, and a mix of the best live bands and most definitive dance music.

As Mo and Tayeb went in, the DJ was fading out the last pre-recorded track before the evening's live show began. It was one minute to twelve. Mo ordered a couple of beers and they sat on a pair of high barstools, giving them a clear view of the stage. Tonight was blues night, featuring the soulful voice of Rashida, the only Arab woman on the circuit.

On the stroke of midnight, her backing group started out with a lively jazzy intro, sustained by a good solid beat. After a few bars, Rashida stepped out into the spotlight, wearing a modest, full-length gown and head-scarf. There was a polite ripple of applause. Her eyes clasped shut in concentration, she let out a long, smooth, musical call – her voice loosening and swelling, searching out the limits of the space.

'Choice, man,' said Tayeb, mostly to himself.

The band kept to the same tune, but gradually slowed and deepened it to the style of rich, southern blues. Then Rashida laid her warm, mellow voice over the music.

> *I feel a swellin' round my stomach,*
> *And an achin' in my breasts.*

> *Woman, quit your moanin',*
> *C'mon girl, give it a rest.*
> *It's the same story, same story,*
> *Same story, same story,*
> *Same story e-very month . . .*

She smiled; some of the women in the audience laughed, others clapped. The blues went on.

> *No man can't find no cure,*
> *No man don't want to know.*
> *He wants you when you're hurtin';*
> *But when that blood begins to flow . . .*
> *(And, sisters:*
> *That's when I want it real bad!)*
> *Help me out here sisters!*
> *It's the same story, same story,*
> *Same story, same story,*
> *Same story e-very month . . .*

Most of the women at least mouthed along with the chorus. There were sporadic shouts of encouragement from every corner of the club. The blues went on.

> *If a man could bear a child,*
> *If a man could feel our pain,*
> *He would start to understand*
> *Why we say it again and again . . .*
> *(But he can't, so he don't,*
> *And he won't, which is why . . .)*
> *It's the same story, same story,*
> *Same story, same story,*
> *Same story e-very month,*
> *Same story e-very month!*

She finished the song on a long, high note, which was covered by a loud burst of applause.

'Give me a little rhythm here!' Rashida called out, after pausing for breath. The drummer obliged by tapping out a steady, laid-back pattern on his snare. Rashida swayed in time to the beat, sliding her way into it.

'Thank you,' she said softly into the microphone. 'Thank you very much. The words of my next song were written by a very good friend of mine, Eleanor Rose Johnson. Eleanor was a black woman poet who died on the fourteenth of January nineteen eighty-eight, aged twenty-four, in police custody. She had committed no crime, and nobody could ever tell me exactly what happened to her.'

Rashida looked slowly from left to right over the hushed crowd and breathed in. The pianist hit the opening chord and she started to sing.

> It isn't like it was,
> Is what my father says.
> It isn't like it was,
> My mother says so too.
> But I say:
> It's not like it will be,
> It's not like it will be,
> It's not like it will be . . .

Most people in the club were well into her show but, more than anyone else, Tayeb was absolutely entranced. It was the first time he had ever heard the blues sung right – which has got to be an event in anybody's life. And on top of that, he was gazing at this incredible, talented, gorgeous young Arab woman.

Rashida finished the first half of her set at about a

quarter to one. Tayeb stood on the footrest of his stool, clapping and whistling. She disappeared off as the dance music came back up for the interval.

The music was too loud for Mo and Tayeb to really talk to each other and neither of them felt like dancing, so they just sat drinking their beers and soaking up the atmosphere.

'I've gotta take a leak!' Mo shouted over the music, and headed for the gents.

Tayeb wasn't listening. He was thinking about Rashida, wondering whether she might go for a boy like him, wondering whether she went for boys at all. By the time Mo got back, he had buried himself deep in a corner of his imagination, where he was slowly lifting Rashida's gown and slipping off her headscarf. Hearing his name spoken, Tayeb unwillingly returned to reality.

'I said, do you want another beer?'

'Sure,' he shrugged.

Mo could see that Tayeb was going down with a severe case of *lurve*. He smiled and shook his head, then leaned across the bar and waved a ten-pound note at the nearest member of staff. The dancefloor lights and music started to fade again as the barmaid went to get their drinks.

Rashida let rip with her own simmering version of *I Heard It Through The Grapevine* and the temperature rose by several degrees. A group of admirers gathered at the front of the stage, clicking their fingers in time to the beat. Tayeb picked up his drink, slid off his stool and went and joined them.

'Feel the heat in that beat,' Mo murmured approvingly.

Hot as it was, it would only get hotter.

Rabin and Jerry had decided to work as a team that night, and had succeeded in enticing a plump, middle-aged Arab businessman back to their lair. Finsbury Park tube station was under a minute's walk away – even for a little person – but they had travelled home in style. The client had paid for a cab, and Rabin and Jerry had perched on the fold-down seats, their backs to the driver, making appealingly lascivious faces at him.

The businessman seemed nervous, which was not unusual, but he should have started to relax by now. He kept on looking like he was about to say something. Every time, they leaned forward attentively – only to see him slip back once more into uncomfortable silence.

'There's no need to be embarrassed,' Rabin reassured him in his best tart's voice. 'We aren't shy and we offer every specialist service.'

He coiled his arms around the man's neck and rested his chin on his shoulder. 'Go on, whisper it to me,' he said huskily.

He pressed his ear up against the Arab's blubbery lips. A moment later, the businessman mumbled out his secrets, fast and low. Rabin smiled and widened his eyes.

'Ooh! That sounds *so* exciting. I tell you what, we'll slip next door for a second or two and give you a chance to get ready. Don't worry, we aren't going far.'

He took Jerry by the hand and led him into the kitchen, discreetly sliding the door shut behind them. They could hear the client panting through the partition as he reached down to pull off his shoes and socks. Rabin opened tbe baby fridge and took out two cans of lager. He pressed one firmly into Jerry's hands and cracked open the other.

'I don't want any,' hissed Jerry.

'I think you're gonna need it,' said Rabin, taking a big gulp.

'Why . . .? Oh, you mean *need*.'

'Yeah. And he wants it in the nude as well, so we'd better start stripping.'

Once they were completely undressed and had swallowed the last drops of beer, they slid open the door and padded softly back into the room to encounter their waiting client.

He lay on his back, sprawled across the shimmering plastic sheet which covered their mattress, wearing nothing but a pair of skin-tight, latex briefs. He writhed in excitement when he saw the naked midgets return.

'Tie me,' he groaned, 'tie me down.'

Rabin secured his hands to a pipe running along the head of the bed with a short length of rope. Jerry chained his feet to a hook which was bolted into the kitchen doorframe, just above the skirting board. The man tugged helplessly against his shackles, thrilled to discover that now there could be no escape.

Each midget straddled one of his fat, hairy thighs and started to piss, spraying warm, salty urine over his chest and stomach. His body convulsed with tingling pleasure. He arched his back and let his mouth fall open. Rabin directed his jet past the man's begging lips. He drank it down, gurgling happily as his swollen prick throbbed and strained against the confines of his tight rubber pants.

It couldn't last for ever, and since their reserves were beginning to run dry, Rabin reached down and caressed the man's crotch until he shot his load into the sweaty latex pouch. They left him tied up, cooling off, and went back out to get dressed.

'What a jerk,' said Rabin, digging another beer out of the fridge.

'Total loser,' sighed Jerry, buttoning up his shirt.

'But not a total loss,' Rabin grinned, holding up a monogrammed leather wallet, fully lined with twenty-pound notes.

'How good do you think we were?' he continued, open-ing the wallet.

'About a hundred quid good, I reckon,' Jerry modestly suggested.

Rabin counted five notes out of the wallet.

'And I'm sure he'd want to leave a reasonable tip – say, another twenty each?'

'Very reasonable,' Jerry agreed as Rabin extracted another two notes.

Rabin clipped the wallet shut and stuck their money in the cookie tin; then he lit a cigarette and went through to the bedroom, slipping the wallet back in the client's inside jacket pocket.

'You will untie me now, please,' said the Arab, having quite recovered his senses. 'I must go now.'

'In a moment,' Rabin said distantly, kneeling by the mattress. 'There's just a couple of things I simply have to know . . .'

He waved the orange tip of his cigarette carelessly across the man's chest, singeing a couple of the longer hairs.

'What do you know about the murder of a Jewish child last night in an Arab-owned shop in the Paddington area?'

The man squirmed. His balls had started to itch madly as the spunk dried into his pubic hair. He was desperate to get his pants off and scratch, and it was getting very difficult to focus on anything else.

'I – I don't know,' he stammered.

'How about an educated guess, then,' Rabin suggested, his cigarette still hovering dangerously.

Jerry stood in the kitchen doorway, swigging his beer and laughing to himself. He *loved* that boy.

CHAPTER 6

The uniformed police had finished roping off the wreckage of the mobile church and had managed to clear one lane on the Bayswater Road. Commander John Deakes from the local force was supervising operations in a distant, bad-tempered way. He stood in front of the ice rink with Inspector Mercer from the Anti-terrorist Squad and Superintendent Woods from the Area Major Investigation Pool. They were waiting for the forensic team to finish raking over the ashes.

'OK, we'll take it from here,' said Mercer, when they finally got the all clear from forensics.

'We'll see to it,' said Woods.

'You leave it to us, Commander,' Mercer continued, turning to Deakes. 'It looks like a terrorist job.'

'Not all serious crimes are perpetrated by terrorists, Inspector,' Woods countered. 'This one's ours.'

'Explosions, *Superintendent*,' Mercer stressed ironically, 'are not generally caused by your common or garden villain.'

'You're out of line, Inspector.'

'Let's face it – we can't afford to risk having your dozy amateurs screw everything up.'

'The last thing we need is your paranoid stormtroopers tilting at windmills and masturbating over conspiracy theories.'

'Say that again,' hissed Mercer, flushing red in the face.

'And you'll piss in your pants? Go ahead.'

Commander Deakes placed his large hairy hands on the back of their necks and prised their faces apart. He spoke in a low voice, addressing nobody in particular.

'I want a full report on my desk first thing tomorrow morning. I shall be holding a press conference at twelve noon and I want the full picture by then. Understood?'

The two men nodded dumbly. Deakes strolled over to his car, climbed in and drove away. Mercer rummaged in his trouser pocket and pulled out a ten-pence piece.

'Toss you for it?'

'Tails,' said Woods.

One of the windows high up on the eighth floor of the block of flats opposite was open an inch. A powerful directional microphone stuck out through the gap, pointing down at Officers Woods and Mercer. Hidden in the shadows next to the window frame sat Isaac, wearing a set of headphones wired into the back of the microphone. He grunted and sniggered as he listened to the policemen bickering. Then he remembered Josh was dead.

'Get on with it, cunts,' he muttered.

Mercer flipped the coin. It went in the gutter. They both scrambled for it.

'Tails!' Woods shouted triumphantly.

'All right, all right,' Mercer conceded gracelessly. 'The first sniff of terrorist involvement, you call me, right?'

'Of course. Now run along, Inspector.'

Mercer stamped off a little way, turned, flicked a V sign at Woods's back, then called his men over to their jeep. They took off at high speed, lights flashing, siren blaring.

Isaac lifted the phone by his side and dialled Trix.

*

Leon and Rachel were relaxing in their dressing room after the last strip of the night. Rachel stared blankly at the wall while Leon rapidly built a spliff. He lit it, drew deeply and passed it to Rachel. There was a knock at the door.

'Yes!' Rachel shouted excitedly.

Trixiebelle squeezed into the room, holding a fake onyx, old-fashioned-look telephone on a long cord.

'Shit,' said Rachel; she had thought it was their dealer.

'It's for you-oo!' sang Trixiebelle, handing the phone to Leon.

He took it off her and listened as Isaac told him what had happened to Josh and the church. He didn't say anything; he couldn't think of anything to say. When Isaac rang off, he slowly cradled the receiver and sat there in silence.

'Not bad news, I hope?' Trixiebelle asked with nosy concern.

'Nothing to worry you,' said Leon.

'I see,' she sniffed, grabbing up the phone and flouncing heavily out of the room.

The door slammed shut behind her, shaking the mirror right off the dressing table. It landed with a thud on the carpeted floor, luckily unbroken.

'Rachel, Josh has been killed,' said Leon.

'How?' she asked, after a long pause.

'Someone bombed out the church – that's what they reckon.'

'Oh.'

'Isaac wants us to tell Jerry and Rabin. He said they'll be at Changes. He'll meet us there later.'

Rachel had let the joint go out. Nothing happened when she drew on it this time. She reached for the box of matches and relit it. Then she started to cry.

'C'mon doll, that isn't gonna help,' said Leon, reaching out and clasping one of her hands firmly in his. 'Let's get this shit off our faces and get going.'

'OK,' she snuffled.

Leon picked up the mirror and they went to work on the facelift make-up. It came off in hard dry flakes, like king-size facial dandruff. Then they got changed. Leon finished dressing first, in a tailor-made, powder blue lounge suit. He went to call a cab and get their night's money off Trixiebelle, leaving Rachel struggling into her peach satin cocktail dress.

A taxi drew up by the entrance to Changes, and Rabin and Jerry jumped out. Rabin stood on tiptoe and stretched his arm through the window to pay the driver. It had been a good evening, so he gave a big tip. The cabbie took the fare in silence and drove off in a hurry. The two midgets were wearing brightly patterned Lyra cycling shorts and scoop-necked vests. They walked into the club arm in arm, and headed straight for the dancefloor.

Rashida had finished her set a few minutes earlier. The music was pounding; the light show was dazzling. Jerry and Rabin had plenty of cash in their miniature bum bags and enough space on the floor to dance without being trampled on. They immediately gave themselves up to the fabulousness of it all.

Tayeb finished his seventh bottle of beer and tried to figure out how best to make his move on Rashida. He was sure that she was still in the club, but he felt too shy to go backstage and ask for her. He hoped that she would come out front, then maybe he could buy her a drink or something. He got up to go to the toilet, stumbled and nearly fell. Mo caught hold of his arm.

'Are you all right, man?'

'Yeah, yeah – I'm great!' shouted Tayeb, swaying drunkenly from side to side.

Rachel and Leon finally made it to the club. They went through to the back, where they found Jerry and Rabin chilling out in one of the booths, sweat pouring off their bodies.

'Hi kids, sit down,' said Jerry, shifting over to make room for them.

Leon told the others what had happened to Josh. They huddled around the table, taking it in, all thinking the same thing: as of now, they were in the firing line. Nobody gave a damn about Dexter's son, but Josh was one of *them*. They had to do something.

'Who is fucking with us?' Rabin wanted to know. 'I should've set that Arab git on fire, not just singed a few hairs.'

'What would've been the point?' sighed Jerry. 'He didn't know anything.'

'I'm sure Isaac'll have a plan,' said Leon. 'Let's see what he says when he gets here.'

It was agreed. They all started to relax a bit, now that they had put off thinking directly about Josh's death. Rachel offered to buy a round of drinks and ambled away in the direction of the bar.

The music went down low and the lights dimmed for the regular *cool half-hour* between two thirty and three a.m. It gave the customers the opportunity to get their breath back for the *last chance rave* from three to four, when the club closed for the night. Mo and Tayeb could talk easily again.

'Let's have another drink,' said Tayeb.

'No way, man.'

'Why not?'

'You're pissed, innit.'

Tayeb thought about ordering himself one anyway, but he didn't reckon it would go down too well with Mo. He decided to change the subject for now, and return to the issue of more beer later.

'That shitty old bus really blew, didn't it? I bet you could've heard it from Shepherd's Bush to Marble Arch.'

'Sweetest sound I ever heard,' Mo smiled. 'We can check our scorecard in the morning paper.'

'You what?'

'Dead and injured, man. We must've got the preacher – I dunno who else.'

Tayeb nodded uneasily. He hadn't really considered that aspect of causing explosions until now.

As they were sitting on tall barstools, they didn't notice Rachel standing next to them. Her head was on a level with their knees and she had been having trouble getting served. More out of boredom than anything else, she had started eavesdropping on their conversation and now her ears were burning red hot. She took a deep breath to steady her drug-frayed nerves and walked slowly back to the booth. When she got there, Leon shook her arm and clicked his fingers in front of her face.

'I think you forgot something, sweets,' he coaxed. 'Do you remember about the drinks?'

He gestured apologetically to the others. She sat down heavily next to him, trying to get her mouth to work. He put his arms around her and gave her a cuddle.

'It's all right, Rachel, don't worry about it. She can't always cope with things,' he explained.

'I've seen them,' she said at last.

'Seen who?' asked Leon.

Having got the first few words out, the rest came more easily, her speech accelerating and fast becoming incomprehensible as she tried to tell him how there were these

Arabs at the bar, and what they had said, and where she had been when she heard it and –

Leon cut her off by putting his hand over her mouth. He stood up and looked around the bar. There was nobody there or, at any rate, nobody even the slightest bit Arabic-looking. He shook his head to Jerry and Rabin and sat back down.

'OK, baby, you're safe – it was just bad thoughts. They've gone away now. Jerry, do you know where I can score some morph?'

'I did see them, I did, I did!' Rachel squealed.

Leon slapped her round the face a couple of times, just hard enough to bring her back down to earth. She burst into tears and clung to him, sobbing like a little girl.

Mo and Tayeb were on their way out of the club. Tayeb wanted to get another round of beers in and go looking for Rashida. Mo swore blind that she had already left while he was in the toilet. Tayeb didn't altogether believe him, but he didn't feel up to an argument either.

The bouncer opened the door for them. Mo said goodnight to him, turned and walked straight into Isaac, who was coming in. Isaac stood in the doorway, rubbing his bruised chin. Mo kicked his dead leg about, trying to get some life back into it.

'Why don't you watch where you're going, you clumsy black bastard!' yelled Isaac.

'Fuck you, freakoid, you nearly got me in the balls man,' Mo spat back.

'We don't encourage racist or sizist remarks in the vicinity of this establishment,' the bouncer said quietly, stepping in between them.

He was at least three shades darker than Mo. Isaac looked a little embarrassed – but only a little. The bouncer let him through into the club and ushered Mo and Tayeb out on to the pavement. Satisfied that he had defused the situation, he followed Isaac in and closed the door.

Mo let out his breath in a long, low whistle. 'How d'you like that? A brother, man.'

He kissed his teeth disapprovingly, then threw an arm round Tayeb's shoulders. They wandered off in search of a night bus to take them back into the West End.

Isaac quickly located the midgets' booth, drew up a chair to the end of the table and sat down. Rachel was still whining and snivelling next to Leon.

'What's the matter with her?' Isaac asked roughly.

'I saw them,' she answered for herself. 'Two Arabs.'

'She's well out of it,' said Leon.

Ignoring him, Isaac grabbed one of Rachel's arms and spun her round. He looked deep into her eyes.

'Go on.'

'These two Arabs at the bar, they said they did it.'

'Did what?'

'Killed Josh.'

She burst into tears again.

'There weren't any Arabs,' Leon said impatiently.

'Yes there were – I could've had the bastards! Shit!'

They all turned to look at Isaac, who was thumping on the table like a madman.

'Let's go! They've got three minutes on us at the most!'

'I'd better take Rachel home,' said Leon.

'All right,' said Isaac. 'Jerry, Rabin, come on – move it!'

They jumped up, sending empty bottles and glasses flying off the table. A few people glanced over at them, then quickly turned back to whatever they had been doing before.

'What do they look like?' asked Jerry, as the three of them raced across the dancefloor.

'Young, Arabic . . .' Isaac hesitated. 'I'll know the fuckers when I see them all right.'

They made it to the exit and waited for the door to be opened. The bouncer recognised Isaac from before and could see he was in a hurry, so he took his time over letting them out.

'Thanks for nothing,' Isaac grated.

'Pleasure to be of service, boss,' the bouncer replied, slamming the door behind them.

'Would you be kind enough to call a taxi for me?' asked a soft, feminine voice.

The bouncer turned and smiled.

'I'd be glad to, Miss Rashida.'

'Thank you. I'll be going to Notting Hill.'

She was tired. It had been a long set. She wanted to be lying in a hot bath at home. She didn't know where her next job was coming from and she didn't want to think about it. She lit a cigarette and sat down to wait for her cab.

CHAPTER 7

Rashida dug herself out of bed at her usual time of eleven the next morning. She washed and dressed, then fixed a pot of real coffee in the tiny kitchen alcove of her studio flat. While the coffee was percolating through, she did a couple of basic breathing exercises then sat cross-legged on the floor, relaxing and trying to meditate. After a minute or so she gave up, stood up – and lit a cigarette.

'God knows there's a limit,' she said to herself. 'You *know* there's a limit,' she added, looking up through the low ceiling towards the heavens.

She sat down with her coffee and cigarette at the desk-cum-dining table in the middle of the room, looking from the blank pages of her diary to the silent phone, then out of the window. She toyed idly with the idea of slitting her wrists but thought better of it.

'If I ever do, it isn't going to be in a *cold* bath,' she decided.

Her flat had running hot water in the evenings but not during the day, owing to an undiagnosed quirk in the immersion heater. Or at any rate, her landlord had never bothered to get it fixed.

She opened the notepad on her desk and jotted down a few ideas for a song. But it was hard to concentrate on composing. A lot of people had failed to come through on their promises and, at this rate, she was going to have to start scratching around for a day job again.

'Merciful Allah, keep me from the evil of telesales,' she

pleaded, only half-joking. 'So much lying for so little money . . .'

The phone rang. It was right next to her but she let it ring on for a while. She didn't want anyone to think she was waiting desperately by the phone. Four rings was as long as she dared put off picking it up.

'Hello?'

'Hello, hang on a tic . . .'

The voice at the other end hesitated. She didn't recognise it, which was probably a good sign. She could hear some pieces of paper being shuffled about.

'Sorry, love. Is that Rashida, Queen of the Blues?'

'This is Rashida, yes.'

'Great,' continued the pie-and-mash voice, without much conviction. 'My name's Harold Drinkwater, I'm manager of the Jolly Roger in Stoke Newington – you've probably heard of us . . .'

He left Rashida a second or two in which to agree. She didn't take him up on it.

'Well, anyway, we're one of London's leading pub-music venues and we're having a festival of local rock talent tomorrow night. You do sing classic rock ballads, don't you?'

'I'm very happy to,' answered Rashida, grimacing at the thought.

'Good. You see, one of my bands dropped out, so I thought I'd give you a chance. If you want it.'

'I could certainly consider it, Mr Drinkwater. What kind of fee were you thinking of?'

'Well now, say you do half a dozen songs. It'll be a great showcase for you – you'd be on early, off home early . . . I can run to a tenner for expenses, and free drinks all night.'

'Can you provide a decent pianist?'

'Hang about – I thought you worked alone.'

'That's all right, I can do. And I don't drink. And it's very short notice. So let's call it twenty pounds for the set.'

He thought about it. Rashida could hear the low-level hiss of him thinking about it, right along the telephone line.

'OK, it's a deal. Just be here by half past five.'

'See you at five thirty tomorrow night.'

He rang off. She put the phone down and breathed a sigh of relief. That took care of food for the week, at least. Now there was just the recurring nightmare of the rent to deal with.

She opened her mail. All one letter of it. The blue phone bill went straight in the bin – there was no point even thinking about it before it turned red. She poured the other half of the two-cup pot of coffee and went back to work on her new song.

It was almost midday.

Commander John Deakes strode into the press briefing room and sat down heavily on his chair. Its tubular metal legs buckled gently with fatigue and he sank slowly downwards until his chin was resting on the edge of the table in front of him. He rolled his eyes heavenwards, taking in the stack of microphones which now sprouted over his head. He thought about his pension, which was only eighteen months away. Eighteen months seemed like a very long time.

Fortunately there was no one else in the room. He got up, exchanged his chair for one of more robust construction and sat down again, rather more carefully this time. His uniform was covered with cat hairs. It annoyed him – the cat annoyed him. When he finally retired it was going. There would be no excuse for it any more. His wife wouldn't be able to pull that *needing a companion while you're out on duty* crap, she'd have a companion: him.

The door swung open and two young constables marched in, disturbing his reverie. He looked at them blankly.

'It's twelve o'clock, sir,' stated the taller of the two. 'Shall we let them in?'

'I suppose so,' the commander said wearily.

The journalists shambled in and sat down, pulling the chairs out of the neat rows in which they had been arranged. Once they were settled, Deakes read out a brief statement covering the essential facts: a privately owned bus had been destroyed by an explosion in west London with one dead and several slightly hurt, and the police were continuing with their investigation.

'I have nothing further to say at the present time. Any questions?'

'Was it a terrorist attack?'

'I'm not ruling out any possibility at this early stage.'

'How close are you to tracing those responsible?'

'No comment.'

'Commander,' one of the tabloid hacks asked with a yawn, 'any comment on the press coverage so far?'

'Yes, as a matter of fact I have . . .'

He held up a copy of the reporter's morning paper. The headline read COMMANDER DEAKS ON TRAIL OF BAYS-WATER BUS BOMBERS.

'It's this sort of sloppy journalism that brings the tabloid press into disrepute,' he continued, pausing for effect. 'It's Deakes with an *e*!'

The journalists laughed and groaned. They were beginning to get restless. The wine bar across the road was calling to them.

'All right, lads, that's your lot,' concluded the ageing policeman. 'Some of us have a job to do.'

They piled out of the room – there was going to be quite a crush at the bar. And they only had four or five hours to turn a bland police non-statement into real news.

Isaac had not attended the press briefing. He had gone to meet Dexter instead.

Dexter sat staring over the rim of his coffee cup into the middle distance. Just below his field of vision stood Isaac, sinking into the shag pile as he made his latest report.

'Is that it?'

'Yes, sir.'

Dexter dropped his eyes and looked directly at Isaac for the first time. With a short, violent flick of the wrist, he flung the remains of his coffee at Isaac's face.

'How could you lose them, you fool?' he snarled.

'We got unlucky,' said Isaac, wiping his face with the back of his hand.

'Then go and get lucky – soon.'

Dexter pressed a button on his intercom.

'Miss Holmes, will you show Mr Hamilton out, please?'

As the door closed behind them, Dexter started scheming again. It seemed that Aziz was not keeping his part of the bargain. He was almost certainly shielding the murderers. He had to be made to understand that it was not in his best interests to harbour terrorists. The only question was how to do so without provoking open warfare.

Emmy, Leon and Rachel had gone over to Jerry and Rabin's flat to play poker while they waited for news from Isaac. They had just finished a nineteenth low-betting hand when the dwarf shoved his way into the room.

'Full house,' said Jerry, squatting down in the kitchen doorway.

'He's not a happy man,' Isaac began.

'I couldn't give a shit,' said Rabin.

'Shut up,' Isaac told him, through clenched teeth.

'Kiss my ass.'

Isaac reached out and smacked him across the face instead. Jerry started getting up but a warning glance from Isaac sat him back down again. Emmy pushed his little round glasses up on to the bridge of his nose and opened a leather-bound document wallet. He clicked the end of his silver-plated ballpoint pen in and out a few times, then coughed lightly. When he finally spoke, it sounded like he had somebody's fist clenched round his throat.

'The fact remains,' he said, as if replying to some kind of coherent argument, 'that I am out of a job, and that we are all in danger until such time as these youths are apprehended.'

'Congratulations, Professor – you figure that out all by yourself?' sneered Isaac. 'You've been going through the books, so what've you turned up?'

'Well, a great deal and not very much.'

'What's that supposed to mean?'

'The church was not terribly popular, as you know, but I haven't been able to tie the two boys you described into any of the known groups that opposed us. Their names would be helpful there, of course – '

'If we had their names, we wouldn't be farting about like this, you shit-for-brains number-fucker!' barked Isaac.

'I'll take that in the spirit of love and respect in which

I'm sure it was intended,' said Emmy, who had a flair for compromise.

'What are we going to do?' asked Leon.

They all looked at Isaac – even Rabin, who had spent the past four or five minutes looking anywhere but.

'The main problem,' Isaac observed, 'is that I'm the only one who really knows what they look like. So, until I think of something better, you lot are going out on the streets with cameras and notepads. You follow anyone who might fit the description, find out who they are and where they live, and get a mugshot. Then you come back to me, I develop the photos and we see if we've got our boy.'

'We should have a result inside of six months,' grumbled Rabin.

'Have you got a better idea?' Isaac challenged, just about holding his temper for once.

There was a long silence.

'Let's get on with it,' Jerry muttered resignedly. 'Spying on them beats the hell out of pissing on them.'

CHAPTER 8

Mo and Tayeb knew they'd been lucky to get the night bus straight away. They just didn't know *how* lucky.

Tayeb slept right through until two in the afternoon. When he saw what time it was he realised that he was going to have to get up, however rough he felt. He threw off his duvet, wrapped a towel round his waist and headed for the bathroom.

After a few minutes under the shower, he started feeling better. And he started thinking about Rashida again. He couldn't believe that he hadn't made a move on her the night before – but then he didn't have a lot of experience with women. Or at least that's what he would have said, but he had to admit to himself that, in reality, not a lot meant none at all. Maybe she was a total bitch, or a dyke, or married . . . He shook his head wearily as he turned off the shower.

'I'm just gonna have to find out, innit.'

He wanted Mo's advice on how to approach the situation but he didn't want to ask for it. He wasn't sure that Mo knew much more about women than he did, anyway. And he knew instinctively that friends, especially old friends, are more of a hindrance than a help when it comes to making the right impression.

He went back into his bedroom and stuck on a cassette. The first two beats of the track rapped out loud and pure before his mother's voice started screeching over it from downstairs. Tayeb punched the wall, hurting his fist, and turned it down. The screeching stopped instantly. These days, it was pretty much the only way his mother could communicate with him.

Tayeb sat on the end of his bed and looked around the room. He hated what he saw. He hated the model planes on top of the cupboard, he hated the tasteful lampshades and wallpaper his mother had chosen. The only things he liked in the room were the tape player and his clothes. He imagined taking Rashida back there.

'Shit, man, humiliating or what . . .'

He didn't want to think about it. He stood up and pulled a tracksuit out of the pile of clothes on the floor. Once he was dressed, he headed downstairs to get some juice. The phone in the hall rang as he went past.

'Yo.'

'Tayeb? It's Mo.'

'Who is it?' Tayeb's mother shouted from the kitchen.

'It's for me!' Tayeb yelled back. 'Sorry about that, man,' he continued into the phone.

'No trouble. D'you want to meet up in a bit?'

'Sure. Anything special?'

'Maybe. Meet me at the Basement in an hour.'

'OK – I should make it.'

'See you there, then.'

'Yeah.'

They hung up. Tayeb went on through to the kitchen and made straight for the fridge.

'Good *afternoon*,' his mother said pointedly.

'There's no juice,' said Tayeb, banging the fridge door.

'Who was that on the phone?' asked his mother, trying to make conversation.

Tayeb's father had died just a year earlier and, although Tayeb was too young and too wild for the job, that still made him man of the house. Neither he nor his mother knew how to cope with the situation – and that made them almost hate one another.

'It was Mo, all right?' Tayeb answered defensively.

He went to the end of the kitchen table where his grandmother was sitting and kissed her on the forehead. She smiled. She always smiled – it just happened to be the expression the stroke had set on her face. Every day Tayeb waited a moment to see if she would say something, but she never did.

'I'm going out,' he announced on his way back out of the kitchen.

'Will you be home for supper?' his mother called after him.

'I dunno. See you whenever.'

The front door slammed shut behind him. His mother sighed and glanced up at the clock on the wall. It would soon be time to feed Granny.

The Basement was pretty much empty in the early afternoon. There was a white studenty couple, their blonde hair knotted into Afrocentric plaits, a Twiglet-thin black guy who worked the coffee bar, and Mo. The short end wall opposite the bar was alive with spray paint. New customers were encouraged to sign in by tagging a clean space on it. The two long walls were lined from floor to ceiling with books by African, African-American and African-British writers.

Mo was flopped out on a giant bean bag in one corner of the underground cafe library, a book propped open on his knees. He was roused from his dream of an Agadir he had never seen by a train rumbling overhead into Holborn Viaduct.

The white couple had started dancing to Salif Keita, who was wailing softly out of the speakers behind the bar. They danced like hippies, feet glued to the floor, waving their arms randomly at each other. Mo went back to his book. At least they were trying.

Four of the midgets had crammed on to a single seat at the back of a Circle Line train headed west, clutching their brand new cameras and notepads. The fifth, Rachel, was taking a photograph of them. The train had been stuck at Baker Street for more than a couple of minutes, but she was still having a tough time holding the camera steady.

'Come on, Rachel, I'm getting squashed,' moaned Emmy, who hadn't really been into the idea in the first place.

'Get up on the shelf, then,' said Leon.

'Yeah, that'd make a really nice com-po-si-sition,' Rachel decided.

Emmy climbed up and sat on the shelf above the seat, dangling his legs over Leon's shoulders. Jerry and Rabin leaned in from either side and Rachel put her finger on the shutter release. The fully automatic camera clicked away happily until it ran out of film.

'Shall we take another photo now?' asked Rachel.

'I think you've used up all your film, sweets,' said Leon.

'I can't have, I've only done one,' she argued.

'Let's leave it for a bit.'

Leon didn't fancy trying to explain how the camera worked.

Rachel sat down sullenly. Isaac had said you push the button and it does all the rest for you, and that it would take thirty-six photos. It must have been a short film or something, she guessed.

The doors hissed and clumped shut.

'There's one!' shouted Emmy, pointing his camera into

the eastbound train that had pulled up alongside. He clicked the shutter just as their train moved off.

'I think I got him,' he smirked, then looked down to see Jerry and Rabin knotting his shoelaces together.

'And we've got you!' they chorused, giggling madly.

Something flashed in Tayeb's eyes. He glared at the seat opposite. It was empty. He figured it must have been a spark thrown up by the other train setting off.

The intercom buzzed.

'This is your driver. I'm sorry about the delay but we've got a passenger on the tracks further up. Well,' he laughed, '*bits* of passenger would be nearer the mark . . . Hang about! I've got a green light. OK, let's go! If it gets a bit bumpy going into Euston Square, you know why . . .'

The intercom clicked off and they pulled out of the station. The combination of the bumpy ride and thinking about Rashida gave Tayeb a hard on by the time they arrived at King's Cross. He readjusted his boxer shorts as he got up to get out.

'Think about something else just for a minute, can't you,' he muttered to himself, as he vaulted the unattended barrier.

Mo was just ordering another coffee at the bar when Tayeb arrived.

'Hi there, man. What d'you want?'

'Milkshake – chocolate. How're you doing?'

'I'm cool,' said Mo, paying for the drinks.

They went and sat on a pair of cushions by a low table at the far end of the cafe.

'You got anything planned for tonight?' asked Mo.

Tayeb shrugged.

'I've got plans. We're going to need proper plans from now on.'

'Whatcha talking about, man?'

'The Jew is strong and cunning,' Mo explained. 'If we're going to carry on with what we've started, we're going to have to do it right or we're going to land in some deep shit.'

'Uh-huh,' Tayeb grunted uncertainly.

'Palestine shall rise up and devour Israel. In the fullness of time, Africa and the old world will destroy the new world of Europe and the United States, and Jewish domination will be ended for ever. Here too, we can participate in purging our land of the Zionist infection, by striking at the very heart of Israeli occupation.'

Tayeb looked blankly at Mo, then looked away. He took a long suck on his straw, wondering what on earth they were talking about. He always felt stupid next to Mo – like he never understood anything that really mattered.

'I don't get it,' he said finally.

Mo drained his cup of coffee and stood up.

'I've gotta go now. I'll meet you at ten o'clock tonight in the kebab and pizza joint on the corner of Piccadilly Circus.'

'Sure, but – '

'Just be ready for anything, OK?'

'It's important, right?'

Mo nodded.

'Well, OK then.'

CHAPTER 9

By midnight, the junction where Stamford Hill rises off Stoke Newington High Street was already pretty quiet. By two in the morning, it was deserted.

On the stroke of two, a low rustling and clanking sounded through the graves of Abney Park Cemetery. An ancient drunk, crashed out in the sheltered entrance to a family tomb, woke up in a cold gin sweat. He crossed himself, said three Hail Marys, then sank back into the folds of his heavy coat and went to sleep.

Two ghostly apparitions bobbed up from behind a gravestone near the cemetery gates.

'All clear,' whispered Mo.

'Uh-huh,' Tayeb confirmed.

They ducked down again, put on floppy white caps to match their overalls and walked out of the graveyard on to Stamford Hill. Tayeb was carrying a pair of two-gallon plastic water tanks; Mo had a bulky holdall and a large pot of black paint. Now that they were out of the cemetery, they looked as unremarkable as a couple of decorators moonlighting for extra cash.

Tayeb stood at the kerb, put down the tanks and rubbed his chafed hands together.

'Time?' asked Mo.

'Two oh five.'

'Let's get to it.'

Tayeb picked the tanks back up and they went diagonally across the junction, up along Cazenove Road.

'Where're we going, man?' he asked Mo.

'It ain't far.'

'What ain't far?'

'Where it's at,' Mo answered flatly.

Tayeb gave up. He couldn't see why Mo had gone all secretive on him, and it was making him edgy. Unlike Mo, he hadn't read the complete set of guerrilla manuals on *effective military command.*

Mo signalled with his head. They turned right down Alkham Road and circled round into a short tree-lined close. Opposite was a large grey institutional building with a gated courtyard to one side. It looked like a primary school, but the small notice outside read Centre for Hebraic Research.

'That's our target,' said Mo.

'What is it?'

'A centre for Jewish propaganda and indoctrination, a filthy hole of – '

'OK, OK – so what's the plan?'

Mo realised that they had reached the point where Tayeb did *need to know*, if he was going to do his part of the job properly.

'You're carrying four gallons of meths,' he explained. 'We're gonna torch the place.'

'OK,' said Tayeb. 'It's empty, right?'

'What?'

'There ain't nobody home?'

'Take a look, man.'

Tayeb looked and listened. All the windows were dark, and no sound came from the building.

'All right – let's get on with it,' he said finally.

'First we've gotta get inside,' said Mo.

They went up to the twelve-feet metal gates, which were chained and padlocked shut. Mo unzipped the holdall and took out a set of borrowed, heavy-duty wirecutters and a large cotton duster. He positioned the jaws of the cutters over a link in the chain and held them there.

'OK, man, you wrap the cloth round the head of the cutters and hold on to it.'

Tayeb did as he was told. When he was ready, Mo pulled the handles together. The cutters broke the chain with a dull clunk.

'Cool, man, cool. Now keep a hold of the two ends while I get these things out.'

Tayeb held the chain while Mo carefully extracted the cutters and laid them down. They slid the chain noise-lessly off the gate, gave it a gentle push, and they were inside the courtyard.

They made for the far corner, where an extension had been added to the original building and where they couldn't be seen from the street. Mo put his hand over Tayeb's mouth, strained his ears and ran his eyes up and down four storeys of plate-glass windows. There was still no sign of life.

'Time?' asked Mo, liberating Tayeb's mouth.

'Two nineteen.'

Mo opened the holdall again and dug out a one-and-a-half-kilo barbell weight. He wrapped it up in the duster and took a firm grip.

'This is gonna sound a lot louder than it really is,' he warned Tayeb.

He swung the weight around and smashed it through the window next to them. It was loud, all right – but the noise of breaking glass faded fast, and there was no alarm. Mo had checked for a box outside and there hadn't been one, but he didn't trust Jews to do things like normal people.

Reaching past the jagged shards embedded in the

frame, Mo unlatched the window. He took out a flashlight and shone it about inside, revealing a kind of meeting hall with stacks of plastic chairs in the corners.

Signalling the all clear, Mo jumped down into the hall. He gathered the equipment together as Tayeb passed it to him through the open window. Last came Tayeb himself, dropping cat-like on to the wooden floor.

Mo touched him lightly on the shoulder as he stretched back up.

'OK, man?'

'Yeah, sure.'

'Cool. Time?'

Tayeb looked at his watch for what seemed like the five hundredth time.

'Two twenny-seven.'

'All right,' said Mo. 'Now we've gotta find the basement.'

'Why?'

'That's where we're gonna start the fire.'

'Why not right here?'

'We've gotta give ourselves time to get away, innit. Let's go.'

They went over to the double doors opposite and eased them open a crack. The corridor outside vanished into darkness at either end. Mo shone his flashlight up to the right, illuminating an open stairwell. This was going to be even easier than he'd thought. They picked up their gear and moved on out.

The stairs led down to another corridor. The first two doors along it were locked. Mo swore under his breath and tried a third. As if the magic words were *fucking motherfuckers*, that door opened on a simple turn of the handle.

The beam of Mo's flashlight swept across the room. It

was piled full of clothes. In front of a heap of unfashion-
able men's jackets was a piece of cardboard on which
someone had written THESE CLOTHES ARE DESTINED FOR
THE USE OF IMPOVERISHED MEMBERS OF OUR COM-
MUNITY – DO NOT TOUCH.

'Should've said do not *torch*,' smiled Mo. 'This'll do just
fine.'

They each grabbed one of the tanks and set to work
drenching the room with meths. As soon as the containers
were empty they backed out into the corridor, choking on
the rising fumes.

'Got a match?' gasped Tayeb.

'Time?' asked Mo, ignoring his question.

'Two thirty-six.'

Mo squatted down and rooted through his bag, retriev-
ing two large paintbrushes.

'Bring the paint, man.'

He hurried off up the stairs, with Tayeb trailing after
him.

Back in the hall, Mo took the paint tin from Tayeb and
prised off the lid.

'Watch this.'

He dipped his brush in the paint, went over to one of
the walls and started painting up and down, then side to
side.

'I can't see anything in this light,' Tayeb complained.

'Hang on a sec.'

Mo finished his design, stepped back and turned his
flashlight on it. Tayeb gasped.

'It's a swastika!'

'Yeah – and it's gonna throw the dogs right off the scent.'

Tayeb looked unsure for a moment. Then he got it.

'Wicked, man, wicked,' he laughed, picking up the
other paintbrush.

When Mo decided they had done enough in the hall, they continued working out along the corridor. Once they had made their way back down to the clothes-filled room, he called a halt to the painting. He opened the door and threw in the brushes, the empty plastic tanks and the paint can.

'Time?' asked Mo.

'Two forty-eight.'

'In exactly five minutes, we drop the match. That gives us seven minutes to get from here to the stop on Church Street to catch the night bus, which leaves on the hour. When we get on the bus, keep your head down, show your pass real clear, go to the front of the top deck and sit under the video camera, where it can't see you. Now we wait.'

Just to be ready, Mo started rummaging through his bag to find the matches. He was disturbed by a strip light flickering on overhead.

'Tayeb . . .!' he hissed angrily.

Tayeb hadn't moved. At the end of the corridor stood a tired-looking old man with a thick grey beard, his hand on the light switch.

'Who's that?' challenged the old man, with what sounded like a German accent. 'What are you doing here?'

With the fearlessness of extreme old age, he walked stiffly up the corridor towards them, partially supported by a heavy wooden walking stick.

'We ain't got time for this shit!' Mo shouted, throwing up his hands in desperation.

The amateur nightwatchman moved surprisingly fast. He went straight up to Tayeb and grabbed him by the collar of his overalls. Tayeb tried to wrestle away, but the old man's grip held firm. Using his free hand, he thumped Tayeb across the back of the head with his stick.

Tayeb blacked out and went down – but Mo piled in over him, punching the man in the face and kicking him in the guts. The man staggered backwards, still clutching Tayeb's torn overall collar, and crumpled to the floor.

Mo pulled the wirecutters out of the bag, jumped back over to where the old man had collapsed, and swung the jaws full in his face. His brains burst up the wall just as Tayeb came to. Tayeb watched in horror as the man's limbs twitched randomly for a moment and what was left of his face collapsed limply around the business end of the cutters.

'Whatcha do that for, man?' he groaned.

Mo didn't answer. The moment the old man's spasms died away, he started tugging on the cutters.

'Hey, give me a hand will you?' he called out to Tayeb, who was still lying on the floor, rubbing his aching head.

Tayeb hesitated, then stumbled over and grabbed one of the handles. They both pulled hard. The corpse started to lean forward and pick itself up from the neck. At Mo's command they each planted a boot firmly on either side of its head, then went back to straining on the handles. With a reluctant grinding, squelching sound, the battered face finally relinquished its claim on the cutters. Mo wiped the end roughly on the corpse's jacket.

'Time?' he asked hoarsely.

'Two fifty-five and thirty seconds – shit!' shouted Tayeb.

'Go, go, go!' Mo shouted back, as he slung the cutters into the holdall.

He grabbed the body by the feet and dragged it into the room doused with meths. Then standing just outside the door, his back to the wall, he struck a match and tossed it in. The room went up instantly. Within a couple of seconds flames were licking round the doorframe.

'Time?' asked Mo.

'Two fifty-six and forty-five,' answered Tayeb from halfway up the stairs.

'Run!' yelled Mo, picking up the bag and slinging it over his shoulder.

They ran. They didn't speak, they didn't think. Their whole bodies were dedicated to breathing, balancing and keeping their legs moving as fast as humanly possible.

The last hundred metres to the bus stop was an agony of aching lungs and tortured limbs, but they finally reached it. Alternately gasping and spitting, they stood bent almost double, leaning heavily on one another.

'Two fifty-nine and fifty-six,' Tayeb panted.

The N73 rumbled around the corner and up the street towards them. Mo stuck out one arm to stop the bus, and threw the other round Tayeb's shoulders.

'We made it, man,' he croaked triumphantly, as the bus pulled into the stop. 'We fucking made it!'

CHAPTER 10

'I'm *bored*,' whined Rachel.

'Watch the TV then,' Leon suggested from the settee.

A freshly built spliff dangled from Rachel's lips. Her glazed-over eyes stared vacantly at the screen of Isaac's television set, which was less than six inches away from the end of her nose. A few seconds later, she laughed.

'Oh yeah – I get it.'

'Great,' yawned Emmy.

Jerry and Rabin carried on playing rummy at the table, silently laying down their cards, shuffling the pack and redealing. They weren't playing for money, so there wasn't anything to make a noise about.

The early morning news started up. Rachel leaned forward and turned the sound right down. The bathroom door sprang open and Isaac clumped out for the third time that night. Once again, he threw a set of useless, dripping-wet prints at the person who had taken them. They hit Rachel soggily on the back of her head.

'Fucking fuck-all use bitch!' he shouted, before stamping back into the bathroom-darkroom and slamming the door behind him.

Time passed.

Leon found himself starting to fall asleep. He went over to the table and laid out a gram of speed on the spare joker. Jerry dealt him in on the next hand. Every now and then, each of the three rummy players dabbed a sticky finger in the little pile of white powder. They were buzzing nicely by the time the bathroom door opened again.

'Emmy!' roared Isaac.

Jolted awake, Emmy's head jerked back and his legs shot straight out in front of him. He slid down and out of the chair and landed on his arse with a thump. Isaac threw a photo in his lap.

'Your roll, print number one. Name and address?'

Emmy reached for his Filofax. Then he looked at the photo and put it away again. The picture was mostly of his own flashlit reflection in a tube train window. But in the background, he could make out the features of a young Arab sitting in the train opposite.

'Ah, I see,' Emmy began, before drying up completely.

'Who the fuck is it?' demanded Isaac.

Emmy started to explain how he had never had the chance to follow the person to find out that sort of information. He was about to describe the circumstances in detail when Isaac pushed the rest of the photos into his open mouth and held them there.

'Shut the fuck up,' he snarled at Emmy, who was gagging noisily on the fixer chemicals.

'At least we all get to see what the guy looks like,' Leon observed.

Isaac grunted and let Emmy go. He spat out the stack of photos, dived into the bathroom, stuck his mouth under the cold tap and turned it on full blast.

While Emmy choked and spluttered into the sink, Isaac passed the photo round the others. Now they had their lead, he figured, it was just a matter of time before they had a real result.

Dexter was already in his office when Isaac called to leave a report on his answerphone. His son's funeral would take up the whole afternoon, so he had got in at seven to clear as much of the day's work as he could before then.

'Progress at last,' he commented drily. 'Go back to work. Success today would double your bonuses.'

He hung up and turned his attention back to reading and signing his way through the mountain of documents his secretary had typed up the evening before.

By the time Dexter had finished with these, Miss Holmes had arrived. She brought him a cup of coffee, his agenda for the day, and her early morning manner – which drifted over the office like a cool, antiseptic wipe. He was grateful for the coffee.

Isaac didn't really approve of recreational drug taking, but he had a brand new sixteen-hour deadline and no energy left to meet it. Once he had finished on the phone to Dexter, he went back to the bathroom and locked himself in.

The mirrored front of the cabinet above the basin lifted straight off its hinges. He laid it over the toilet bowl, then turned back and reached up behind his shaving kit on the top shelf. From there he retrieved a small self-sealing polythene bag containing about three grams of ninety per cent pure cocaine and a clean razor blade. He cut just one short line before putting the bag away.

'Just wanna jump, just wanna fly,' Isaac snuffled, as his nose trailed evenly across the mirror.

A loud banging started up in the back of his head and spread through his brain like wildfire. He took a deep breath of cool air, sucking it up into his mind, where it extinguished the blaze at once. His consciousness floated gently on the steam clouds, then blew straight forward into sharp, bright focus.

The banging started up again – but now it was outside, behind him, on the bathroom door. Isaac rinsed the mirror off and rehung it, then threw back the bolt and shoved open the door. Emmy jumped to his right. The edge of the door clipped his trailing left foot, sending him into a spin which ended abruptly with his face slammed up against the skirting board.

Isaac didn't see Emmy go down, so he thought he must have just fallen asleep in front of the bathroom door.

'Wake up, there's work to do – now!' he barked.

Emmy didn't move – not even when kicked – so Isaac bent down, grabbed a fistful of his wispy hair and dragged him up to a sitting position. A couple of hefty slaps brought him back to his senses.

'I want to be somewhere else,' Emmy said ponderously, sucking back the blood and saliva which had collected at the front of his mouth.

'Too bad,' Isaac retorted.

'What's the score?' asked Jerry.

'We've gotta nail the Arab today. No more time.'

'Fucking great,' said Rabin, throwing down his cards.

'There's an extra fifty per cent all round,' Isaac continued, enthusiastically upping his own bonus by three hundred per cent.

'OK,' said Leon, 'let's hear it.'

'You, my team of experienced sales executives,' Isaac announced, 'will go door to dooring in Bayswater, giving free and very cheap quotes for professional carpet cleaning. Meaning, of course, you have to go all the way round the house, and measure every room. You use my number for confirmation and adopt your usual covers. The name of your company . . .' he paused briefly to think, 'is The Royal Express Cleaning Service. Any questions? No.

Good. Go home now, shave, shower, change into something smart – and be back here by eleven for further instructions.'

Shocked into action by Isaac's uncharacteristic coherence, the midgets hauled themselves together and stumbled out of the flat.

Isaac cleared the table with the back of his hand and sat down with a large-scale map of west London. He selected the most promising area, then started marking out pitches for each of them to cover during the afternoon and evening to come. Once that was done, he'd have to go down to the post office and get some instant business cards made up on the machine there.

'And we'll be up and running by the end of the morning,' he grinned.

Shortly after midday, Dexter's intercom buzzed. He flicked the switch.

'I said no calls, Miss Holmes.'

'Yes, Mr Dexter. Your marketing director wishes to see you.'

'Let him in, then,' he said impatiently.

'Mr Dexter will see you now,' she relayed to Ed King, whose ample figure was already most of the way through Dexter's office door.

'Steven, I'm sorry to bother you at a time like this,' he began, closing the door behind him.

Dexter waved away the apology and motioned him to the chair in front of his desk. King drew the chair right up and sat down.

'I thought you should see this.'

He opened up the early edition of the *Evening Standard* and spread it out under Dexter's nose. Dexter looked at the photo, read the text, then looked at the photo again.

It was a news item about an arson attack the night before, supposedly caused by ultra-right-wing, anti-Semitic extremists. The photograph showed a series of swastikas, clumsily daubed on a crumbling internal wall. The fire had gutted the entire building.

'I sincerely hope that I am not becoming paranoid,' said Dexter.

'Who could blame you? First your son to the Arabs, now the British Nazis – '

'That's not what I meant. Look at the photograph.'

He pushed the paper back towards King.

'I can only see what's there,' King frowned, trying to find something new in the shadows.

'Then look at those swastikas.'

King looked long and hard at the swastikas. They were just the same as before.

'They're back to front,' Dexter pointed out.

'I suppose it must have been a particularly ignorant bunch of Nazis – '

'Though undoubtedly well-organised and effective urban terrorists?' Dexter countered.

'Opportunists, more likely.'

'The report suggests to my mind that the action was thoroughly planned. The swastikas were painted not sprayed, the lock on the gate was cleanly broken, minimal damage was caused on the way in . . .'

'Well . . .?'

'That would suppose at least one intelligent person in command. If that person was a neo-Nazi, I would expect them to know which way round a swastika goes. This attack falls within a pattern of anti-Semitic activity, but not by would-be Nazis.'

King patiently awaited enlightenment, but Dexter had said all he had to say on the subject.

'Thank you for bringing this to my attention, Edward,' he concluded, extending a hand towards the door.

Dexter was certain that his Arab enemies were again responsible. His current approach was proving ineffective, even on a level of simple containment. He had expected the terrorists to drop out of circulation once he had issued his warning to Aziz – but now they were rampaging out of control, unchecked by the supposedly civilised leaders of their community. He decided that some demonstration of the outrage he felt had become necessary. The question of exactly what could wait until after his son's funeral, when his mind would be suitably focused.

CHAPTER 11

Rashida had been expecting a cross between Hampstead Village and the Angel – she had never been to Stoke Newington before. She flip-flopped along Church Street towards the Jolly Roger, feeling the pavement through the thin, leather soles of her sandals. The atmosphere was tougher than she had expected, more real: hope and fear cutting through the blanket depressiveness of the area.

'Bad enough for me,' she smiled.

Behind her, over the noise of the traffic, she heard a slowly approaching shuffle of dozens of pairs of feet. She turned to look.

They came two by two. It wasn't exactly a public procession – they didn't have a licence for one. But over a hundred Jewish men, women and children were marching in angry protest. Out of respect for the law, they kept to the pavement and they kept moving.

Rashida sensed their anger and became suddenly afraid. She fought the fear – the stronger half of the fear and hatred of the Jewish people which her father and mother had handed down to her. She forced herself to stand still and watch until she was calm again. Then she breathed out – she hadn't realised she'd been holding her breath.

The two men at the head of the line carried a banner stating their one demand: END NAZI ATROCITIES IN BRITAIN.

'Can't argue with that,' Rashida said to herself as she crossed the road – not to escape from the marchers, but to make way for them.

The Jolly Roger was just over the next junction. It looked like any other pub with its mock-Tudor facade and rows of wooden tables and benches lined up on the concrete forecourt. The only original feature was the sign over the door – a cheery, cutlass-wielding pirate.

The pub was obviously closed, but half a dozen young men with shaved heads and tight blue jeans were hanging around outside. Two of them lounged on one of the tables, watching the other four play no-rules football with a crushed lager can.

Looks like my gay groupies made it here before me, thought Rashida, stepping over the low chain which separated the Jolly Roger's private slab of concrete from the public pavement.

Then she took a closer look. The youth nearest her had a swastika tattooed behind his ear and a ring through his nose like a bull's. One of the boys on the table had stencilled NF on the thigh of his jeans with an indelible black marker. The other had Thamesmead True Brit printed across the back of his T-shirt. Skinheads.

The football match came to an abrupt halt and Rashida steeled herself against the inevitable attack. But instead of advancing on her they moved off into Church Street, leaving a clear path to the pub's entrance. She followed them with her eyes, as they formed a disorderly line at the side of the street.

'Yiddoes, yiddoes!' they shouted at the passing marchers, punching the air with their fists.

The elders at the front did their best to ignore them, but some of the younger men further back had had enough. The procession ground to a halt as they stepped out of line and collected in a defensive formation on their side of the road.

'Here we go, here we go, here we go!' chanted the skinheads, as Rashida banged as hard as she could on the Jolly Roger's front door.

There was no reply. She quickly glanced around for some other way in. There wasn't any. Out of the corner of her eye she saw twenty or thirty more skinheads charging down towards the pub from the direction of the station. Then she saw the doorbell marked H. DRINK-WATER – PRIVATE. She leaned on it.

The six at the roadside had turned towards Rashida, but they still didn't seem to see her. With almost perfect synchronisation, they dropped their trousers and thrust their bare bottoms in the direction of the marchers. A moment later, they spun around and flapped out their uncircumcised dicks.

'Skins, skins, skins!' they shouted, pointing down at the sorry display of their assembled manhood.

The Jewish men started to laugh, but it died in their throats. The chant of six drunk schmucks pulling up their pants was drowned out by the battlecry of an army of menacing thugs, closing in fast from the left.

Rashida didn't know whether to try and break down the door or just make a run for it. The grinding of heavy bolts followed by the distinctive clunk of a mortice lock provided the answer. She whipped around, jumped through the opening door and slammed it shut behind her.

'Hello Mr Drinkwater, my name is Rashida, I'm pleased to meet you – call the police,' she said, without pausing for breath.

Drinkwater stared at her blankly for a moment, then slowly turned and looked behind him at the clock over the bar.

'You're early,' he grumbled. 'We aren't open yet.'

'Would you call the police, please?' begged Rashida.

'What's the matter, love? You been mugged?'

'There's a riot going on out there!'

'That's funny. I don't hear anything.'

They listened. Silence. Drinkwater went over to one of the windows, pulled back the curtain and peered out.

'All I can see is a bunch of people looking at each other. Ain't no law against that, is there?'

Rashida joined him at the window, climbing on a barstool to match his height. The two factions stood glowering across the street at one another, neither sufficiently sure of victory to start anything. Rashida knew how loaded with tension the silence was – but she couldn't help feeling a bit ridiculous, all the same.

'Sorry, it's just I thought . . .' Her voice trailed off.

'Not to worry, love,' said Drinkwater. 'I'll show you your dressing room. This way . . . Oh, and no feet on the furniture, if you don't mind.'

'Of course – I'm sorry,' Rashida apologised, stepping down from the stool.

She followed him past the small raised platform that served for a stage, then through a door at the back of the bar. It opened into a warm, dimly lit corridor which smelled of fresh country meadows masking stale piss.

'Through here,' said Drinkwater, pushing open a door on the left.

Rashida looked at the brass nameplate. It said MARES. The room opposite was for STALLIONS. She started feeling depressed. This gig had clearly not been blessed by the Fates.

At the far end of the ladies' toilet was the locked door of her dressing room. Drinkwater handed Rashida the key and she wrestled the door open. A mop, bucket and broom fell out at her feet.

'It's a cupboard,' she stated matter-of-factly.

'I'll get these out of your way,' said Drinkwater, ignoring her comment and gathering up the pub's cleaning kit.

Rashida bit her lip. It was time to be all professional, get her bit done with, get paid and go – never to return.

'What sort of a crowd are you expecting tonight?' she asked, wondering which songs to choose from her repertoire.

'Oh, they're a lively bunch – don't need much warming up, if that's worrying you . . .'

He picked up on Rashida's total lack of enthusiasm and changed his tack.

'No trouble – we never have any trouble here.'

He paused, searching for inspiration.

'You're sort of representing the Asian community, if you like.'

'Really? And *who* am I replacing at such short notice?'

Drinkwater scratched his bald patch, smoothed a few long side hairs back over it and cleared his throat.

'The Oi Boys,' he said finally.

'They don't sound like a Bengali group to me.'

'No, well . . . Anyway, I've got to open up, so I'll leave you to it. You've got the best part of an hour to doll yourself up, and if you're anything like my wife . . .'

He laughed with his reflection in the stained mirror over the basin, readjusted his hairs and left.

Rashida moved into the space he had just vacated and stood looking at herself for a little while.

'Right, that's me dolled up for the show,' she sighed. 'Fifty-nine and a half minutes to go.'

There was a chair and an ashtray in the cupboard. She sat down, crossed her legs and lit a cigarette.

Drinkwater flicked a switch behind the bar, illuminating the LIVE MUSIC sign in the window, then went to open the door. Outside, it seemed like time had stopped. He looked at the silent, motionless figures in front of the pub. He couldn't work it out. Normally they were jumping about all over the place by opening time. Slowly an idea came to him.

'Funny half-hour!' he announced at the top of his voice. 'Half-price drinks for half an hour to get the party going!'

He went back in and waited behind the bar. A moment later, in twos and threes, the skinheads sloped off into the pub to get their cheap drinks. When the last one was inside, the Jewish marchers set off again towards Stamford Hill. But the forty-odd young men who had stepped out of line stayed where they were, arms folded, staring at the pub's open door.

CHAPTER 12

An old-fashioned chalkboard next to the Jolly Roger's
door gave a run down of the evening's acts, with Rashida's
name at the top of the list. Tayeb had clocked it the night
before, as he and Mo passed by on their way to the
cemetery. Now he was coming back up on the bus by
himself, feeling tense. In the first place, he wasn't sure it
was a good idea showing his face in Stoke Newington
again so soon. And secondly, he was chasing a date with
the Queen of the Blues herself.

'Loosen up, man,' Tayeb muttered to himself as he
jumped off the bus.

'Fucking shit!' he said out loud, as he looked up.

His stomach twisted into a tight knot the moment he
saw the large gang of mean-looking Jews. They were less
than ten yards away. Tayeb's mind went into overdrive.
He wouldn't stand a chance in a fight. He could run, but
where would he hide? How did they know he was going
to be there? They couldn't possibly know – nobody knew,
not even his mother, not even Mo . . .

He started to calm down. Apart from anything else,
they showed no interest whatever in his arrival. All the
same, he resolved right then and there that he was going
to have nothing more to do with Mo's crazy schemes,
which always seemed to end up with at least one person
getting killed. He felt much better at once – then suddenly the full force of his paranoia came flooding back.
The Jews were watching the entrance to the Jolly Roger.

Very slowly, Tayeb turned around and took exactly fifteen paces away from them. Then he crossed over to the side of the road with the pub on it. Bending down to retie one of his shoelaces, he sneaked another look at the Jews. They carried on stubbornly ignoring him.

'I ain't gonna let them spook *me*,' Tayeb decided.

The sky was grey and overcast, but he slipped on his shades anyway and strode purposefully back towards the pub. Once he was safely through the door, he let out a sigh of relief and pulled off his shades.

'This is not happening, man, this ain't *real*,' he groaned.

A pub full of skinheads in front of him, a street full of Jews behind. That left precisely no place to go.

'I'm here now, innit,' he said to himself, making straight for the bar.

To his amazement, he got all the way there without being lynched. Blanking the vicious looks from all sides, he pulled out a five-pound note and waved it at the fat balding creep behind the bar.

'A pint of lager and a packet of crisps.'

Drinkwater took a long hard look at him.

'Are you over eighteen?' he asked suspiciously.

'What do you think?' said Tayeb.

'I dunno.'

'Course I am.'

'You don't look it to me.'

'That's cos you're a hundred years old, innit.'

'I don't have to serve you, whatever age you are, understand?'

'I get it – you don't serve blacks, right? What is this – the fucking colonial club?'

'Just serve the fucking Paki, Harry!' one of the skinheads shouted from the end of the bar. 'We're fucking dying of thirst over here.'

'You can have a Coke,' Drinkwater decided, 'or you can fuck off.'

'Give me a fucking Coke, then,' hissed Tayeb.

Drinkwater came back with the Coke and a lecture about attitude, manners and respecting your elders and betters.

'Save it, fats,' said Tayeb.

The thirsty skinheads were thumping on the bar. Drinkwater went to serve them. A boy about Tayeb's age, with a fat red boil on his neck, was jostled against him by the crowd. He turned and stared aggressively into Tayeb's face. Tayeb watched the head of pus blossom on his boil. The boy leaned back, spat on the floor in front of him and stomped off. With a considerable effort, Tayeb blanked him. Now was not the time for a confrontation.

'There's a fucking horrible smell round here,' one of the skinheads told his friends, jerking his head in Tayeb's direction.

'Someone oughta clean that up – I don't wanna step in it by accident,' added another.

They laughed loudly – more loudly than even they thought the joke deserved – and ordered another round of Snakebites. Tayeb kept his head down. He knew better than to look at them. He was beginning to wonder how much longer he could put up with it all when Drinkwater announced the first act over the PA.

'Thank God it's her already,' Tayeb murmured into his empty glass as Rashida sat down at the piano.

The skinheads didn't share his enthusiasm. After an initial outburst of low whistles and sporadic shouts, they steadily took up the chant.

'Off! Off! Off!' they chorused.

Rashida let it ride for a while. She sat demurely, back straight, hands on her lap, legs crossed at the ankles, looking out over the piano. After a while of nothing happening, the skinheads began to get bored and the noise level dropped considerably. This was what Rashida had been waiting for. She pushed her voice up and out, rising easily over the moronic chanting with perfectly tuned power.

At first I was afraid – I was petrified!

She hammered out the chords on the piano as hard as she could, drowning out the screeches of derision. By the time she reached the chorus, she was belting out the words like a challenge to a prize fight.

I will survive – I will survive!

Tayeb was loving it, jumping up and down and applauding wildly during the piano solo. Rashida glanced around the audience, spotted him and blew him a kiss. She really appreciated the support just then. Tayeb waved right back.

Rashida smiled, got her mind back in time with her fingers on the keyboard, and launched into another verse.

So now go – walk out the door!

A group of skinheads, tired of heckling, took the hint and wandered out on to the pavement. It was cool and quiet outside. The Jewish men had kept up their silent watch. As the skinheads bundled out of the pub, they advanced a couple of paces into the street. The skinheads didn't like it.

'Fuck off, yiddoes!' shouted one of them, sticking up two fingers for emphasis.

He took a last gulp from his bottle of super strength lager and chucked it across the street. It sailed over the heads of the Jews and shattered harmlessly on the wall behind them. The front row of the formation exchanged glances, then each one calmly produced a full-length hunting knife and held it out in front of him.

For a second, nobody moved. Then the skinheads fell back a few yards towards the open pub door. The Jews took another two steps forward. They were now blocking one whole lane of the street.

An open-top 2CV, driven by a young French woman on holiday, came hurtling around the corner. She slammed on the brakes, pulled down hard on the steering wheel and closed her eyes. The car spun off to the right, down the side road next to the pub, then slewed back to the left and smashed head on into the plasterboard extension which housed the Jolly Roger's gents' toilet. The driver shot eight feet straight up through the open roof and landed back down on her seat, her legs folded in perfect lotus position – stone dead.

The Jews rushed forward to get out of the street. The skinheads misinterpreted this manoeuvre as a full-frontal attack. They threw their glasses like grenades as the Jews reached the near kerb, and hurried back inside the pub to gather reinforcements. One of the glasses caught a young Jewish man on the side of his head. It splintered and opened a three-inch gash across his temple. He sat down on the kerb, shakily picking little shards of glass out of his scalp, while the blood ran down his arm and dripped off his elbow on to the pavement.

The collective attitude of restraint snapped. The rest of the Jews charged over the concrete forecourt and burst into the pub, smashing the wooden door half off its hinges. Rashida stopped singing and ducked behind the piano as bottles and glasses flew indiscriminately across the room. Tayeb vaulted the bar and crouched down behind it. Drinkwater disappeared through the sliding door to the cellar and bolted it firmly behind him. Everyone else in the pub joined in the fight with enthusiasm. Most of them had knives. Those that didn't improvised blades out of broken glasses and bottles. Tayeb reached up behind the bar and pulled a little kitchen knife with a serrated edge out of a heap of lemon slices.

It was six ten precisely when Sergeant Lawton received the call over the police radio in his high speed pursuit car, parked on the corner of Hackney Downs.

'One medium, deep-pan pepperoni pie ready for collection,' said the caller, who had been patched through by the station.

Lawton clicked off the radio and nodded to the constable who was sitting in the driving seat at his side. The constable flipped a switch and turned the ignition key. They roared away up Amhurst Road, lights flashing, siren blaring, accelerating smoothly through the gears to a cruising speed of approximately one hundred miles per hour.

As they approached the junction with Stoke Newington High Street, the constable double declutched expertly and slipped the Rover into second gear, bringing their speed down to a shade under forty miles an hour. Sergeant Lawton glanced to his left as they powered through the red light – but there wasn't even time for him to open his mouth.

The first of a convoy of four identical patrol cars responding to a reported incident in Church Street ploughed into the nearside wing of Lawton's car as it emerged from the side road. The sergeant was killed instantly.

The second and third cars piled up behind. The crumple zones on the first car ruptured, then the whole frame buckled and gave. Its windscreen blew out and the roof folded down on top of the two policemen, who were still struggling to release their seatbelts. The weight of twisted metal crushed their bodies deep into the collapsed front seats.

The fourth car screeched to a halt just in time and immediately started backing away. Then it jumped to a halt, the engine stalled. As the young constable reached forward to restart it, his hand began to shake uncontrollably and he burst into tears. The accelerated promotion for graduate entrants just hadn't come fast enough for him.

There had been fewer deaths at the Jolly Roger, but at least as many injuries. A skinhead stuck the sharp points of his broken beer glass into a Jewish youth's disbelieving face and twisted it firmly. As the youth choked blindly on his own blood, one of his comrades spiked the skinhead clean through the neck with a hunting knife. The skinhead spun around, whipping the handle out of the Jew's grip. He stood swaying from side to side, gasping for breath, clawing at his punctured throat, then collapsed. The Jew pulled the knife out of his convulsing body and looked around for someone else to stick it into.

Rashida had slid down off her stool and entrenched herself behind the piano. She was beginning to wonder how much longer it could stand up to the ceaseless battering.

'Thank God it's an upright,' she said to herself, as another bottle smashed against the back, striking a duff chord.

She knew she was trapped. She just sat there waiting for the police to come in and break it up. Surely somebody had called them, so where were they?

Tayeb was thinking the same thing in his hiding place between the beer crates. But *he* didn't want to be there when the police arrived. He raised himself up and peeped over the bar, ducked to avoid a flying glass, then looked again.

The largest knot of fighting had moved away from the door, over to the stage. Soon, very soon, they would happen on Rashida, forgotten behind the piano. Tayeb felt a tightening in his chest: his fear for her safety. Putting the knife between his teeth, he crawled to the end of the bar nearest the stage and pulled himself up and over. He landed heavily on his backside, roughly cushioned by the flabby white beer belly of a badly cut skinhead. He scrambled to his feet, leaving the skinhead puking over the polished brass footrail.

Tayeb looked around for the best way to get to Rashida. There wasn't one. He was surrounded by warring Jews and skinheads. And he had stood still too long. A Stanley knife slashed through the arm of his baggy tracksuit, just grazing the surface of his skin. Tayeb lashed out with his knife in the direction of the blow. He followed through with the rest of his body to see the blade raking across a skinhead's face, cutting deep through his right eye. The skinhead screamed and fell to his knees, clasping his hands over his face. Tayeb turned back towards the piano. He watched two skinheads grab one of the Jews and ram him up against the back wall of the pub, suddenly opening a clear way to the stage.

'Praise the Lord,' Tayeb whispered in amazement.

He wasn't waiting for a second miracle. With a jump and a roll, he was through the gap and up on to the stage.

A split second later, he was behind the piano with Rashida.

'Time to make a move, sister,' he said breathlessly, taking her by the hand.

Rashida wasn't sure. Two burly Jewish men jumped up at either end of the piano and tipped it forward off the stage, where it flattened the four skinheads who had been using it to guard their backs. Now Rashida was sure. She let Tayeb lead her down from the stage.

Holding her close behind him and waving his knife wildly in front of him, Tayeb backed them along the wall and out through the door to the toilets. They ran straight up the corridor and tried the door marked PRIVATE. It was locked solid.

'I know,' said Tayeb. 'We can get out through the gents' – there's gotta be a window.'

'There wasn't one in the ladies',' warned Rashida, 'and I'm afraid I won't fit through an extractor vent.'

'You might have to,' said Tayeb, grabbing her arm and ushering her into the STALLIONS' toilet.

The place was wrecked, which seemed only natural given the state of the bar. What surprised them was the sight of the 2CV's bonnet sticking through the far wall. They dashed over to it and pushed. For a little while, it resisted their best efforts. Then, all of a sudden, something gave. Several pounds of old plaster dust emptied over their heads, and the car rolled back with comparative ease. As soon as there was room enough to pass, they squeezed out along either side of it.

Rashida paused at the driver's side, admiring the French woman's willpower. How could she meditate so profoundly when she must be in such pain? Then she realised the woman was dead. She shivered and looked around despairingly.

'C'mon, Rashida,' Tayeb said softly, 'let's get the fuck outta this dump.'

He stretched out a hand. She took it and gripped it firmly.

'What's your name?' she asked.

'Tayeb.'

'Don't you think we'd better wait for the police, Tayeb?'

'No.'

The question surprised him. He saw that his answer had surprised *her*. Then he got it – she was just a bit square.

'One, no point – they wouldn't listen to us. Two, d'you reckon they're gonna turn up before we get ourselves killed hanging around here? Three, they might just want to hold us overnight – and I don't fancy sharing a cell with a bunch of psycho fascists.'

'Oh – I see. What do you suggest, then?'

'Get a cab – and now.'

Rashida walked up to the corner and looked to the right. The fighting had spilled out on to the pavement in front of the pub. There was still no sign of the police. She looked to the left. Approaching fast on the other side of the road came the familiar orange sign of a black cab for hire. She waved Tayeb over and hailed it.

Tayeb held his bleeding right arm back, away from the driver. Rashida climbed in.

'Where do you live?' he asked her.

'Colville Terrace.'

'Colville Terrace, Notting Hill,' he told the driver, jumping in next to Rashida.

The cabbie turned off his light, marked up the extras on his meter and drove them away.

CHAPTER 13

'It's right at the far end,' Rashida told the driver as they turned into Colville Terrace.

She glanced over at Tayeb, who hadn't said a word since they got in the cab. She was curious about him, but something set in his expression stopped her from trying to make conversation.

The fare was over seventeen pounds. Tayeb pulled out a twenty-pound note, but Rashida insisted on paying half. They got out and stood on the street corner while the cab turned.

'Would you like to come in and put something on that cut?' she asked finally.

'Thanks,' mumbled Tayeb, looking away from her.

They climbed the whitewashed stone steps to the front door. Inside was a thinly carpeted staircase, leading up to Rashida's first-floor flat. The bathroom was directly opposite as they went in; round to the right was the large studio room where she cooked, sat and slept.

'All yours?' asked Tayeb.

'That's right.'

'Neat.'

'I like it. Why don't you wash that cut out while I make some coffee.'

'Sure.'

'Have a rummage in the cabinet – I'm sure there's some TCP or something,' she added, as he disappeared into the bathroom.

Tayeb shut the door behind him and breathed out heavily. He didn't know what was the best way to handle the situation. She'd asked him in for coffee, so he must be doing all right up to now. But he knew he'd have to start talking soon. The serious, silent bit could only get a guy so far. He splashed some water on his face, then took a look at his arm. It wasn't too bad – just a scratch, really. The tracksuit top was a write off, though. He gazed deep into the mirror over the basin.

'Look, if she likes you, great. If she don't, that's her problem,' he told his reflection.

As she hunted for a second cup, Rashida started wondering quite who she had invited into her home. He could be a thief, a rapist, a serial killer – or a deadly bore.

'Well, he maybe just saved your life, girl, so he can't be all bad,' she said to herself, going over to the stove.

She came back with the full pot of coffee and set it down in the middle of the table. Tayeb was standing in the doorway, leaning on the frame.

'Come in,' she said. 'How's the war wound?'

'S'all right,' Tayeb smiled shyly.

Rashida smiled back. He was quite cute really. And he was nothing like those flabby distant cousins her father was always trying to get her acquainted with. She decided that he definitely was *not* training to be an accountant.

'I really like your singing,' Tayeb said at last. 'You got any tapes?'

'I'm still waiting on that record deal,' she laughed. 'You're not in the business, are you?'

'No.'

Rashida stared out through the window. Somehow Tayeb's presence in the room let her relax, released her from always trying to *do* . . .

She lit a cigarette and drew on it thoughtfully.

'Sorry, would you like one?' she asked, offering the packet.

'Yeah, why not?'

'They give you cancer,' she smiled.

'If nothing else gets you first,' he said distantly.

Rashida struck a match and watched the smooth skin of his face glow as he leaned in to light his cigarette. He was younger than her, but seemed older too – like a child-soldier returned from the front. Then she remembered: Tayeb and another young man, leaving Changes in a hurry, and the little people chasing after them, like in a dream.

'How much trouble are you in, Tayeb?'

'A whole lot.' He surprised himself with his honesty. 'Or maybe none at all,' he added.

'You'll have to tell me about it one day.'

'It's a deal.'

They looked across the table at one another. Rashida reached out and laid one of her hands on Tayeb's. He picked her hand up, intertwining their fingers, and pressed it gently against his forehead.

'A lot of crazy shit going on in there,' he grinned.

'I bet there is.'

The peacefulness of the flat surrounded them, enveloped them, guarding them against any unwanted intrusion from the city outside. Safe in the space they had made for themselves, they leaned forward and kissed.

The Royal Express Cleaning representatives had succeeded in booking a large number of appointments for their non-existent service, but had failed to turn up any new leads in their search for the murderers. Rabin had gone off to turn a trick; Rachel had gone home to sleep off her drug-enhanced nervous exhaustion; Isaac, Emmy,

Jerry and Leon sat around in Isaac's front room, trying to think of what to do next.

'Two fucking hours – then that's it!' Isaac raged, banging his fist on the table.

'We lost our moderate bonuses – the world does not come to an end,' Emmy intoned from the sagging depths of the armchair.

'Shut the fuck up!' shouted the dwarf.

Neither Jerry nor Leon could be bothered to get involved in the argument. They curled up on opposite ends of the settee, shut their eyes and tried to go to sleep. Isaac wondered what he was going to tell Dexter. He wanted to have another plan at least thought out before he spoke to him again.

The phone rang.

'Shit!'

It could only be Dexter, and he had nothing to report except total failure – and no new ideas. He slapped himself across the face a few times to sharpen his concentration, then picked up the receiver.

'What have you got for me, Zak?'

'Nothing definite so far, Mr Dexter.'

'That's not good enough, *is it*?'

'We just need more time – '

'Time? *Time!*' Dexter exploded. 'You have had the time – and the resources – to find Lord Lucan, the Loch Ness Monster and Haile Selassie's grave!'

'I've just started work on a fresh angle,' Isaac lied.

'So have I,' Dexter cut him off. 'And *I* know what I'm doing . . .'

Isaac listened to Dexter's tersely delivered instructions and hung up. He turned to Jerry.

'We've got a little job to do. Call Rabin and arrange a meet – we may need him.'

'What now?' grumbled Jerry, half asleep.

'Just do it!' roared Isaac, lobbing the phone at him.

Tayeb and Rashida sat side by side on the edge of her bed. She leaned lightly against him, her arms wrapped around his waist. He felt the weight of her head on his cheek and let his right arm fall gently across her shoulders. Their bodies swayed slightly with their breathing, rising and sinking together, feeling one another's warmth. Tayeb half coughed, cleared his throat.

'Do you want me to go?' he asked hoarsely.

'Don't be silly . . .'

Rashida tipped her head back and looked up at him. His face was set, expressionless; but his eyes glistened with unspoken feelings, unresolved tensions.

'I want you to stay. Do you want to stay?' she asked quietly, carefully.

He looked down, seeing her again, gazing into her eyes. The vague, formless pressures clouding over him evaporated, driven away by the certainty of her look.

'Yes.'

'Good.'

They kissed. Lying back in each other's arms, they kissed again, their lips moving softly together, sharing the warmth of their breath. Their legs and arms became entwined, their bodies pressed together. As their lips parted, their tongues touched and embraced; searching, finding, caressing . . .

Rashida eased down the zip of Tayeb's shiny tracksuit top, running her fingers lightly through the soft hairs on his chest. He arched his back, slipping the tracksuit off his shoulders and on to the floor, then wrapped his body back around Rashida's, pressing his mouth against hers. As they kissed, Rashida caressed Tayeb's back, her nails circling his shoulders, tingling up and down his spine, her fingertips massaging the soft skin of his lower back.

They rolled over. Rashida gently pulled away, leaned back, and tugged her shapeless gown up over her head and off. Tayeb lay on his back, gazing at her: her delicately curving figure, her coffee-coloured, perfect skin and her silk-white bra and knickers.

'You're beautiful,' he murmured.

'So are you,' she smiled, pulling off his shoes and socks.

She rubbed his bare feet, playing with his toes, then jumped up and dragged his trousers off. His erection bulged against the cotton material of his boxer shorts. Lying down beside him on the bed, she ran her hands softly up and down the length of his body. He reached out and unfastened her bra, caressing her breasts, then her thighs; slipping his hand inside her panties, feeling her damp, curly hair, exploring her with his fingertips. She panted evenly, eyes closed, drawing him towards her, kissing him on the neck, then on the lips . . .

Rashida rubbed her nose against his; he opened his eyes.

'Just a sec,' she whispered, kissing him.

She got up and dug a packet of condoms out from behind one of the books on the shelf.

'I hope these aren't past their use by date,' she giggled.

She went back to Tayeb and gently lowered herself on to him, feeling his stiff cock press into the soft flesh of her stomach. She ran her fingers up and down his thighs, up inside his shorts, lightly caressing his balls. He stroked and kneaded her silk-clad buttocks, then firmly pulled off her panties, slipping his hands between her thighs.

Rashida moaned, then slid halfway down the bed and tugged at Tayeb's boxers. His cock sprang up as she got his shorts off; she carefully rolled the condom on, then pulled herself back up into his arms. Mouths pressed hotly together, their tongues embraced once more, passionately, irresistibly. Rashida guided Tayeb into her; he started to thrust, she wrapped her thighs around his buttocks, moving with him. They grunted together, moved together, thrusting deeper and deeper; Rashida let out a little cry and a gasp, then Tayeb:

'Yeah, yeah, yeah – *yeah*!'

They collapsed together, panting, welded one to the other. Then they kissed again – softly, gently – smiling in one another's face, exhausted.

'I'm in love,' whispered Tayeb, partly to Rashida, mostly to himself.

'I love you back,' said Rashida, kissing him on the nose.

Slowly, reluctantly, they disentangled themselves. Rashida picked up her packet of cigarettes and lit one for Tayeb, then another for herself. She glanced over at the clock. It was almost one in the morning.

They smoked in silence for a while, then Rashida leaned over and kissed Tayeb on the forehead.

'I wanted to ask you something.'

'Like what?'

She heard the defensive tone in his voice and moved closer, wrapping her arms around him.

'I just wanted to ask you to take care of yourself. Will you do that for me?'

Tayeb took a last drag, leaned across Rashida and stubbed out his cigarette. He exhaled slowly, watching the trail of smoke drift away.

'Always have done up to now,' he said.

'Good. Are you sleepy?'

'Kind of – yeah.'

Rashida turned out the light. They snuggled down

under the duvet, Tayeb lying on his back, Rashida wrapped around him. Relaxed and comfortable, they began the gradual drift off to sleep.

The doorbell went. They ignored it. A moment later it went again: three long, insistent buzzes. Rashida opened her eyes and groaned.

'Who the fuck's that?' growled Tayeb.

'Probably my father,' she sighed. 'Or one of his henchmen.'

'What – at two in the morning?'

Rashida forced herself out of bed and put on her full-length gown and headscarf.

'He will have heard about what happened at the concert this evening. He hears about everything – usually sooner rather than later. And he will order me to come back home and I will refuse to go, and we'll have a big row and he will go home by himself. You'd better stay here,' she added, seeing Tayeb sit up.

'OK,' he said, lighting a cigarette.

She hurried down the stairs and opened the front door. Standing at the top of the steps was a prep-school boy, in the St Cuthbert's uniform of navy blue blazer and cap, and grey shorts. He was holding a collecting tin with GRAND ANNUAL JAMBOREE printed on it. The boy rattled his tin and said something very quietly, which Rashida couldn't make out.

'You'll have to speak up,' she said, bending down towards him, thinking all the time how weird the whole thing was – schoolboys collecting at this time of night.

A powerful hand reached out of the shadows and grabbed the back of Rashida's neck, forcing her mouth and nose into a thick wad of cotton wool. The cotton wool was drenched with chloroform. She struggled briefly, and went under.

'Good boy,' Isaac told Rabin. 'Shut the door quietly, then take her legs.'

Tayeb heard the distant clunk of the door closing and waited for Rashida to come back up. Thirty seconds later he was still waiting. He got out of bed, slipped on his shorts and padded softly out on to the landing. Breathing silently through his open mouth, he leaned over the bannisters and looked down the staircase. There was nobody there.

Isaac and Rabin carried Rashida's inert body down the steps to Isaac's Volvo estate. Jerry was sitting in the passenger seat, watching the road in the sunshield vanity mirror. They laid Rashida carefully out in the back and covered her with a rug; their instructions had been strictly not to damage the consignment. Then Isaac dug an envelope out of the glove compartment and went back up to the front door.

Tayeb crept down the stairs. Maybe Rashida was rowing with her old man in the street, like he used to. But he couldn't hear anything through the door. As he stood there wondering what to do, a blank white envelope fell through the letterbox, landing on one of his bare feet. He bent down and picked it up.

'What the fuck?'

Tayeb tore open the envelope. Inside was a printed card. He pulled it out and squinted at the text. He couldn't understand it, but he recognised the characters: Hebrew.

'Motherfucking Jews – *shit!*'

He heard a car engine starting up outside. It seemed to take him for ever to find the lock, turn it back and get the front door open. Then he was out, down the steps and on to the street in a fraction of a second. He saw the rear end of Isaac's car turning north up Ledbury Road. He started to run after it, but there was no hope of catching up. Just before the car disappeared from view, Tayeb glanced at the number plate. He got as far as C699 – then it was gone.

He stared after it for a while, half expecting the abductors to drive back and confront him. But there was nothing. Eventually, Tayeb turned away and slowly retraced his steps. He went into the house, closed the door behind him and leaned heavily against it. There was only one thing he could think of doing now. He ran up the stairs to the flat, grabbed the phone and dialled Mo's number.

After about thirty rings, someone finally answered. Tayeb heard a baby screaming and angry voices shouting in the background.

'Yeah?' Mo said sleepily.

'Mo, it's Tayeb – '

'It's the fucking middle of the night, man.'

'You're telling me what I already know, guy. I'm at Rashida's place.'

'You lose it, man? Tell me about it tomorrow, OK.'

'She's gone.'

'Do what? She walk out on you?'

'No. Listen – there were these Jews . . .'

Mo let out his breath in a long, low whistle. It was starting to happen – just like he always knew it would.

'You safe?' he asked.

'Yeah – I think.'

'Give us the address.'

He grabbed a pen and scribbled down Rashida's address on the pad by the telephone, then tore off the page.

'Ten minutes,' he grunted decisively, and slammed down the receiver.

CHAPTER 14

The Volvo estate drove east along Marylebone Road towards King's Cross, keeping carefully to the speed limit. Dexter had paid for the car to be specially adapted so that Isaac could see over the steering wheel and reach the pedals with his feet at the same time. It was against Isaac's nature to stop at traffic lights just because they were red, but he forced himself. They had landed an easy catch and he didn't want to blow it now.

'Who is she, anyway?' asked Jerry.

'Who cares?' said Rabin.

Isaac had nothing to add. His only concern was the amount of Dexter's money Rashida might be worth.

They took a left up Pancras Road, then turned into a narrow dead-end side street behind King's Cross station. Isaac parked on the right, between an overflowing builders' skip and the burnt-out shell of a Mister Woozy ice cream van. He killed the engine and doused the headlamps. The street was perfectly quiet. Nobody had lived or worked there in months.

Isaac climbed down from the driver's seat and walked a few yards along the pavement. He stopped in front of a windowless red-brick block and unlocked its cast-iron security door.

Rabin and Jerry sat watching for Isaac's signal. When he raised his arm, they jumped out and hurried round to the back of the car. Under the blanket, Rashida was unconscious but breathing normally. They heaved her body out over the rear bumper and lumbered it up to the doorway.

'She's too fucking big,' moaned Rabin.

'Shut the fuck up and get her inside,' Isaac told him.

Inside was a whitewashed brick corridor, lit at regular intervals by red safety lamps. Isaac resealed the entrance while Rabin and Jerry lumped Rashida along to the end of the corridor and down a spiral staircase.

The basement door opened into a sparsely furnished office space, illuminated by a flickering fluorescent tube. Directly opposite was a small, cell-like room containing a bed, table and chemical toilet. Jerry and Rabin took Rashida through, laid her out on the bed and locked the cell door on her.

Isaac fiddled with the controls of a twelve-inch television set on the office desk, trying to get a picture. Fuzzy black and white lines buzzed up and down the screen. He slapped the monitor repeatedly. It crackled and whined, then finally produced a clear image. They could see that Rashida was still sleeping off the anaesthetic.

Pleased with the night's work, Isaac picked up the phone and dialled Dexter's number.

Mo jogged along Colville Terrace, glancing up at the house numbers as he passed. He'd have some explaining to do next time he showed his face at home – but that could wait.

Tayeb was pacing the floor in front of Rashida's window. When he saw Mo coming, he dashed down the stairs and pulled open the front door.

'Good to see you, man – real good,' he said, holding out a hand to Mo.

Mo took his hand and gripped it firmly, looking deep into Tayeb's eyes. He was all right – rattled, but all right.

They went inside, shutting the door behind them. Mo sat Tayeb down on the bottom stair.

'Tell me what happened.'

Tayeb told him everything he knew – which didn't amount to much, since he had been in bed when all the most significant events had taken place.

'But I made part of the plate – C699.'

'What're we gonna do with that?' asked Mo. 'I ain't got no police computer thing.'

He picked up the calling card and examined it: Hebrew, like Tayeb had said.

'I think it means *An eye for an eye, a tooth for a tooth*,' Mo translated.

'How d'you make that out?'

'It's in English on the back.'

Tayeb hadn't noticed the print on the other side of the card. He snatched it away from Mo and read it again.

'Yeah, well – what the fuck does that mean, anyhow?'

'Tit for tat, innit,' Mo explained. 'But you ain't got no idea why – why her?'

Tayeb shook his head: if it had been either of *them*, he would have known exactly why.

'Let's get to work,' said Mo, leading the way up the stairs and into the studio room.

He drew the curtains in the darkness, then turned on the bedside light. He realised immediately that it wasn't a rich person's flat. The Jews weren't after a ransom. But they wouldn't be going around kidnapping people just for the hell of it, either.

'There's gotta be a reason,' Mo said out loud. 'She's gotta be involved in something.'

'She didn't say nothing about anything,' Tayeb protested.

'Gotta be something,' Mo repeated, leafing through Rashida's desk diary.

Every entry seemed to be to do with a gig, or an agent, or a record company. Maybe it was in code or something – there had to be *something*. He finished with the diary and turned his attention to the bookcase.

On the bottom shelf was a thick, leather-bound photograph album. Mo opened it up. The first thing he saw was a black and white picture of a stern, middle-aged Arab man. Written in ink in the bottom right-hand corner was the inscription *To a devoted daughter from your loving father*. He looked closely at the photo. He was sure he had seen the guy somewhere before.

Then it clicked, and suddenly everything made sense.

'Mohammed Aziz,' he whispered. 'Her old man is Mohammed Aziz.'

Tayeb looked up vacantly; the name meant nothing to him.

'He's The Boss,' said Mo. 'He owns the whole of west London. They took her to get at him.'

'So what're we gonna do about it?' asked Tayeb.

'Get outta here for a start,' said Mo, turning off the light and drawing back the curtains.

'Then what?'

'I dunno,' Mo confessed.

'We gotta do something – '

'I'm with you, man,' Mo assured him. 'But we're going to find ourselves playing piggy in the middle to two major league teams, so we're going to have to be *extra* sussed. OK?'

'OK.'

They touched fists.

'C'mon, guy,' said Mo, 'let's go over to your place and make some plans.'

CHAPTER 15

'*Where is my daughter*?' raged Mohammed Aziz.

'She's quite safe,' Dexter replied, with studied calm.

'If she is returned to me unharmed today, I shall take no action, otherwise – '

'No action is not enough!' Dexter cut him off.

The two men stood glowering across the desk at one another, fists clenched. There was a tap at the door and Miss Holmes stepped into the office with the early morning coffee tray. Like a pair of schoolboys caught fighting in the playground, Dexter and Aziz looked away and sat down. Miss Holmes placed the tray in the middle of the desk and marched back out. She was quite certain Mr Dexter hadn't noticed the new shade of lipstick she was wearing.

'I require your assistance in tracking down my son's murderers. When they have been brought to justice, your daughter will be returned to you.'

'You think you can force me to cooperate?'

'I hope to persuade you. Milk and sugar?'

'Neither,' snapped Aziz.

Dexter served himself with both, then settled back in his chair and closed his eyes. Having both might *and* right on his side meant that it was simply a question of waiting for Aziz to capitulate.

Dexter's eyes popped back open as Aziz's hands locked around his throat, expertly shutting off his windpipe.

'You're getting old,' Aziz snarled into Dexter's reddening face. 'You aren't a soldier any more. Why do you seek to provoke a war?'

Dexter's cheeks turned purple. A distant, tickling splutter sounded from deep in his throat.

'Only soldiers prosper in times of war – you must know that.'

The noise from Dexter's throat crackled and faded. Saliva bubbled at the corners of his mouth.

'I will bring you your murderers and you will return my daughter,' Aziz continued, without loosening his grip. 'Then, as we live in a time of peace, you will provide me with a just reparation for this crime against my house.'

Dexter's swollen tongue stuck out between his front teeth. A dark veil fluttered down over his face.

Aziz finally released him. The veil lifted, leaving Dexter bent double in his chair, choking up phlegm and gasping for breath. Aziz turned away in disgust, snatched up his briefcase and stormed out of the office.

A diamond-white stretch limo was illegally parked right in front of the entrance to Dexter's building. The liveried chauffeur who came with the car stood on the pavement nearby. When he saw Aziz come out, he snapped to attention and opened the back door for him.

As the Mercedes pulled away from the kerb, Aziz began to relax into the soft leather upholstery. He even started to see the funny side of it – of his nearly strangling Dexter to death, that was. As for his daughter, he reasoned, she was probably safer in Dexter's protective custody than she was in one of her nightclubs. What annoyed him was the thought that with more foresight – or by exercising more control over his daughter's wayward ideas of independence – he could have prevented Dexter from gaining this tactical advantage.

Aziz picked up the carphone and dialled his office. His deputy, Abdul Shahabi, took the call.

'Abdul, this is Mohammed. I want you to assemble a committee for direct action, chaired by yourself and reporting to me. The committee will, as a first priority, locate my daughter and carry out an exact assessment of the defences behind which she is held. As a second priority only, the committee will discover the identity and whereabouts of the murderer or murderers of David Dexter and then move to detain them. Any questions?'

'When can I expect a full briefing?'

'As soon as your committee is assembled.'

The limousine drifted along Moscow Road, past the entrance to Guildford Mews. In the smallest bedroom of the house on the corner, two young men were formulating their own plans for direct action.

'We ain't getting anywhere, man,' groaned Tayeb.

They had been up all night. Countless mugs of coffee had kept them awake but cut a ragged edge on their nerves.

'We ain't got anywhere to go,' grumbled Mo. 'We don't know where she's at, where the Jews are at, where The Boss is at –'

'You ain't trying, man!' Tayeb exploded.

'Look, guy,' said Mo, gripping Tayeb's shoulders, 'I know you're mad, but that ain't showing us the way – so just chill out, all right?'

'I'm cool,' grunted Tayeb. 'Just tell me what to do.'

But Mo didn't know what to do. That was the problem. 'I'm thinking,' he lied.

Mo tried to think. He lay back on Tayeb's bed, screwed his fists into his eyes and tried.

Tayeb slapped a tape into his Walkman, stuck the headphones on and pressed play. Peak volume hip hop bounced across his brain, blasting out any possibility of

conscious thought. Mo tried shaking the blankness out of
his head. He succeeded in making himself feel a bit dizzy,
but no new ideas came along. The rattle and hiss leaking
out of Tayeb's ears started to irritate him. He wanted to
know why he always had to be the one to come up with
everything, when it was Tayeb's girl who was in trouble.
He wasn't about to get his throat cut on *her* behalf, that
was for sure. Then inspiration struck.

'Hey, I think I've got something . . .'

He sat up and looked over at Tayeb, who couldn't hear
him through the music. Mo felt like stamping on the
Walkman. Instead, he reached across and snatched the
headphones off Tayeb's head.

'Whassup, man?' shouted Tayeb, trying to grab them
back.

'I said, I've got something,' Mo repeated, stopping the
tape for good measure.

'Yeah? Like what?'

'An idea, maybe.'

'OK – shoot.'

'All right,' said Mo, now he finally had Tayeb's attention. 'Here it is: we throw in with The Boss.'

'Do what?'

'We go and see Aziz, and tell him what we know, and
say we'll help him get his daughter back.'

'I ain't going near that motherfucker.'

'S'all right,' Mo shrugged. 'I'll go for both of us.'

'That ain't it, man. It's like, Rashida told me she doesn't
want nothing to do with him, right? And if he found out
about me and her – I mean the shit would hit!'

'I ain't telling.'

'OK, but – she said he finds out about everything.'

'Well, if that's the case, then you'd better start watching your ass, cos he's gonna be coming after you, man.'

Tayeb hadn't figured that out before now. He tore the empty cigarette packet into little pieces, then stood up and started pacing around the room. As he passed the bed for the third time, Mo caught his arm.

'Siddown, man.'

Tayeb sat on the floor at the end of the bed. Mo climbed down next to him. They sat shoulder to shoulder, staring out into space. Eventually Mo broke the silence.

'Listen, man,' he said. 'We're gonna need protection, whichever way you look at it. And our best bet has gotta be going with Aziz. If we help him out now, then he owes us, right? And if we want to win the war and get your girlfriend back, then we're going to have to work with him anyhow, cos we can't do it on our own. If we don't, then we're just going to be waiting for him to come round here and break your butt.'

Tayeb nodded. There didn't seem to be any way around it. Mo stretched out one of his arms and laid it across Tayeb's shoulders.

'So maybe we're gonna be getting ourselves into some real dangerous shit here,' Mo admitted, 'but at least you and me is in it together.'

CHAPTER 16

Rashida was wrenched awake by being suddenly and violently sick. The spasms in her stomach dragged her up to a sitting position as she vomited down the bedsheet over her knees.

Isaac's anxious face was fixed in front of the monitor. The corners of his mouth relaxed and spread into a relieved grin. He had begun to think he might have overdone the anaesthetic and put her under for good.

'When she's finished, I'll pop in and say hi,' he decided.

In the mean time he swung his feet up on top of the desk, cracked open another beer and leaned back to enjoy the rest of the show.

'Oh – my – God,' moaned Rashida, as she choked up the last little stubborn bits.

Everything kept shifting around her. She closed her eyes again and tried to concentrate. Her eyelids felt sticky, like the lashes were brushed with glue. Where in hell was she . . .?

She pulled the soiled sheet away, leaned back against the wall and tried looking again. This time nothing moved. With a little effort she managed to focus on the low wooden table, the door, the big plastic box in the corner . . . She looked back at the door. There was no handle. Her gaze drifted slowly upwards. In the corner above the door was a closed-circuit camera, looking right back at her.

'That kind of shit,' she sighed.

She could still taste puke in her mouth and smell it in her nose. It was depressing, but it meant she was alive. And that meant whoever it was wanted her to be alive – which also meant they wanted her to *stay* alive. She committed this fact to memory: it might well come in useful.

Now that Rashida's mind was starting to warm up, all the memories of the night before came flooding back: the gig, the riot, the dead girl, the schoolboy-midget, Tayeb . . . She wondered if they'd got Tayeb, what he'd done, why they'd kidnapped her, where she was . . .

The sound of a key being turned in the lock broke her train of thought. The door opened and Isaac shambled into the room. He had always been squat and ugly, but the combination of class A drugs, no sleep and too much to drink rendered him actually repulsive. Rashida recognised him at once – he was the one giving the bouncer a hard time at Changes. She huddled herself into the far corner of the bed, waiting to see what he would do. Isaac looked at her curiously, then gathered up the dirty sheet and turned to go back out.

'You must be hungry after all that, eh?' he said. 'I'll fix us some dinner.'

He turned his head to take another look at her and winked knowingly. Then he went out, taking care to lock the door securely behind him.

The thought of food and the sight of Isaac made Rashida feel sick again. She fought it back down and concentrated on trying to pull herself together. Swivelling on her hips, she managed to get her legs dangling over the edge of the bed. Then she pushed herself gently forward until the soles of her feet touched the floor. Very slowly, she raised her body up, as if embarking on a daredevil balancing act. She sat down again. The next time getting up was a little easier. She shuffled away from the bed, just making it to the wall opposite. After resting there for a moment, she shuffled back. Her thighs and calves ached painfully, but she was happy just to be able to feel them again.

Isaac was in the small kitchen area attached to the office. He took four pre-packaged Whole Meals out of the fridge and stuffed them in the microwave. When they were ready, he tipped three of them out on to one plate and the fourth on to another. Then he grabbed a handful of cutlery from the drawer and took them through. The large portion he left on the desk in the office, the small one he carried through to the cell.

Rashida made sure she was back in her original place on the bed by the time Isaac got the door open. He dumped the plate down on the table, together with a knife and fork. On second thoughts he picked the knife back up, smiled paternally at Rashida and left the room, locking it as before. She leaned forward and inspected the meal: a dreary heap of green lentils and rice in a watery sauce. She ate a mouthful to get rid of the taste of sick, but that was her limit.

Isaac was happily shovelling his dinner down his throat when the phone rang. He swore long and loud at Dexter for interrupting his meal, spraying lentils in all directions. Then he picked up the receiver.

'Yes, Mr Dexter?' he inquired politely, now that his mouth was empty.

'Change of plan, Zak. I am no longer convinced of the security of this location. You will move the hostage tonight.'

'Where to?'

'Place of safety six – understood?'

'Gotcha.'

'You will take the greatest of care.'

'Yeah, yeah.'

'Very well, then. See you anon.'

'You what?'

But Dexter had already rung off. Isaac slammed down the phone and went back to his food. He glanced over at the monitor and saw that Rashida wasn't eating.

'Not fucking good enough for Princess Arab-Bitch, huh?' he muttered darkly through his last mouthful.

He picked up his empty plate and threw it in the wastepaper basket; he wasn't paid to wash up. Now the beer was all finished, he could feel a monster hangover coming on. He jumped up, stamped over to the cell door and let himself in.

'Whassamatter with you, then?' he demanded.

Rashida didn't know what he was talking about, but she decided it was probably best not to say so. Instead she gave him her very blankest expression and said nothing.

'Dontcha speak English, bitch? Is there a fucking problem here?' Isaac continued, jerking his head in the direction of the virtually untouched Whole Meal.

Rashida suddenly realised that she must have offended him by refusing his cooking. It was such a ridiculous idea that she almost wanted to laugh, but she could see he was quite serious.

'I'm sorry, I'm afraid I'm really not very hungry,' she said apologetically.

'I'll make you fucking sorry!' Isaac raved, punching the wall hard enough to bruise his knuckles.

Rashida shrank back, but Isaac calmed down again almost at once. He even smiled at her.

'You don't like all that veggie shit, right? A lady like you needs a bit of meat, right?'

He fingered his crotch suggestively. Rashida did her best to hide her fear and disgust, and made a pretty good job of hiding the fear – thus displaying her disgust all the more clearly. Isaac went cold with anger, and the anger made him feel powerful.

'Betcha only go for dark meat – that's it, ain't it?'

Rashida looked down to avoid meeting his gaze. Isaac clamped one of his hands round her chin and pulled her head up.

'Betcha think I've got a real tiddler, seeing as how I'm so fucking short, eh?' he rasped. 'Big mistake, bitch!'

'I wasn't – '

'Shut the fuck up!'

He released her chin and drew his arm back to smack her across the face. But he kept just enough of a grip on himself not to do it.

'Don't want it to show, do we?' he muttered. 'But you're gonna feel it all right, oh yeah – better believe it . . .'

As he spoke, he undid the top of his trousers and let them fall around his ankles. Isaac didn't go in for under-wear. He flopped his large, semi-erect penis straight out on to the table.

'Look at that and tell me it ain't gonna be a tight fit,' he challenged.

Rashida looked, summoned up all her reserves of strength, and plunged her fork right through the middle of his swollen member, deep into the wooden surface of the table. Isaac squealed in agony. He stood pinned to the table by his rapidly deflating penis, watching in shocked disbelief as blood streamed out through the puncture holes.

Rashida seized her chance. She dashed out of the cell and across the office to the door opposite. It was locked.

She was still feeling faint and nauseous but she forced herself to hold it together. Glancing quickly back around the room, she saw that Isaac had left the key in the cell door. She threw herself at the door, slammed it shut on his back and locked it. Then she launched into a frantic search for the key that would open the door to the outside world.

The desk yielded nothing but a few sheets of paper, a half-eaten packet of extra strong mints and a well-thumbed copy of *Penthouse*. She tried the kitchen area. The shelves were bare and the cupboards were empty. With a growing sense of hopelessness, she tried the fridge. Inside were three more packet meals and half a pint of sour milk – but no keys.

A sickening wave of fatigue swept over her. She stumbled back into the office and sat down heavily behind the desk. Swallowing hard to keep the little she had left in her stomach where it was, she leaned back in the chair and tried to think sensibly. What could he have done with the keys?

As she rocked back and forth to ease her churning guts, she heard the distinctive clinking of metal on metal. She twisted her neck to look behind her: slung over the back of the chair was Isaac's check sports jacket.

'How could you miss it, fool?' she muttered, pushing herself to her feet and hurriedly going through the pockets.

She ran to the door with a handful of different keys she had found and started trying them out. On her fifth attempt, the key turned in the lock and the door swung open.

Shaking with nervous energy, Rashida started up the spiral staircase. It was hard work and, exhausted and dizzy as she was, she could only take it a couple of steps at a time. She rewarded herself with a little rest after every advance, pushing on again as soon as she got her breath back.

Leaning heavily on the handrail, she rounded the final bend and clambered up the last few steps to the top. Now she *had* to sit down. Her eyes started closing by themselves, but she fought to keep them open. Resting back on her elbows, she made herself look up along the corridor. The line of soft red lights seemed to stretch off for ever.

Rashida sighed heavily. She wasn't out of it yet. The dwarf was probably capable of tearing both doors off their hinges and coming up after her. She shuddered at the thought and dragged herself to her feet.

As she struggled along the corridor away from the staircase, she heard a rattle and clunk. A moment later, a large rectangle of bright, white light opened up in front of her. She started hurrying awkwardly towards it, but her legs felt impossibly heavy. The white light folded away into the shadows and disappeared.

'I'm afraid we can't let you leave us like this.'

It was Emmy's voice. He stood a few feet in front of her, arms folded, blocking the way. Rashida lunged forward, hoping to shove him aside and escape.

She fell heavily. Jerry had wrapped himself around one of her legs; Rabin held on tight to the other. She had no strength left to fight the three midgets. Emmy recovered the keys from her, then they half carried, half dragged her back down to the basement office.

'Where's Isaac?' Emmy asked Rashida, as they laid her out on the desk.

'In there,' said Jerry, looking at the monitor and pointing at the cell door.

Rabin went over and unlocked it.

'Knock, knock!' trilled Emmy.

But Isaac didn't reply. His shoulders were hunched and taut, his head hung down, and his knuckles were dead white from holding on to the table.

Rabin moved past him into the cell. Then he saw the object of Isaac's distress.

'Ooh!' he winced. 'You do that for kicks, Ike?'

'What's up?' asked Jerry.

'Come and take a look,' said Rabin.

Jerry took one look at the burst blood sausage sticking out from under Isaac's shirt and called over to Emmy for the first aid kit.

'Get ready to catch him,' he told Rabin.

Rabin positioned himself behind Isaac and held out his arms. Jerry climbed up on to the table, grasped the handle of the fork with both hands and pulled.

As the fork came out, Isaac groaned and collapsed back into Rabin's arms. Rabin swung him round and dropped him on to the bed. He was out cold.

Emmy hurried in with a selection of lint dressings and a large bottle of antiseptic solution. He pulled back Isaac's shirt and poured a generous dose over his bloody genitals.

Isaac came straight back to life, roaring with pain and wildly flailing about with his fists. The midgets hastily retreated into the office and locked the door on him. The patient clearly wasn't ready for treatment.

Emmy went back up the stairs to check the outer door while Jerry and Rabin settled down to the task of guarding Rashida. Jerry took out a pack of cards and dealt a round of pontoon; Rabin skinned up a joint.

Rashida stayed where she was on top of the desk and tried to rest. Keeping every movement as small as possible and breathing silently through her mouth, she concentrated on tensing then relaxing her body, one muscle group at a time.

I got one thing right, she thought wearily. *I'm still alive.*

CHAPTER 17

Abdul Shahabi had assembled his committee. The four wise men he had chosen were all senior executive officers of Aziz's finance and property empire. Their anti-Zionist credentials were unimpeachable, their loyalty to Aziz absolute.

The committee members quietly discussed the state of the economy, the company's performance within it, and possible strategies for the future. They all agreed that Aziz's plans for the business could not be improved upon, but each executive saw a special leading role for his own department.

Silence fell as Aziz entered the room. He was accompanied by two uniformed security guards, who scanned from floor to ceiling for electronic listening devices. Once they had certified the room clean for use, Aziz dismissed them and delivered his brief.

'So, gentlemen,' he concluded, 'what are your initial proposals? Firstly, for the safe recovery of my daughter.'

The committee members coughed, shuffled the pieces of paper in front of them and stared thoughtfully into the middle distance.

'Progressive economic sanctions?' suggested one.

'We are pressed for time,' Aziz responded coldly.

The executive looked back down at his pad and doodled a swirl of razor wire along the top of the brick wall he'd drawn earlier. Shahabi cleared his throat.

'It appears to me,' he said, 'that the only way to ensure

her *safe* return is to comply with terms, and focus our attention on item two, the detention of the undesirables.'

'I will not be dictated to by a Jew!' ranted Aziz. 'This is not a committee for compromise – it is a council of war. What is your experience of developing counter-insurgency strategies? Anyone?

The prolonged, embarrassed silence was finally broken by a knock on the door. A male secretary entered the room and handed a piece of paper to Aziz. He cast an eye over it and stood up.

'When I return, I shall require a solution,' he threatened.

The secretary held the door for Aziz, then followed him through to his office.

'Show our visitor in, then stay and take notes,' Aziz told him.

The young man brought in by the secretary marched straight up to the desk and stood to attention. Mo was wearing black and white Nike trainers, black jeans, black bomber jacket, baseball cap and mirror shades.

'Well?' said Aziz.

'I am an Arab soldier,' Mo announced.

'Is that so?'

'Yes, sir.'

'What are you doing here?'

'Serving the interests of our Arab nation. Our enemies must be destroyed.'

Aziz looked Mo up and down, then turned to his secretary.

'Thank you, Hassan.'

The secretary folded his pad and left the office.

'At ease, soldier.'

Mo stood with his feet apart and folded his arms across his chest. Aziz leaned forward over the desk and lifted off his shades. They looked each other straight in the eye. Aziz frowned.

'Why might I want to enlist the services of a juvenile mercenary?' he asked carefully.

'To get your daughter back.'

Aziz's eyes widened perceptibly. Mo's face remained a mask.

'What do you know of my affairs?' demanded Aziz.

'Your daughter was taken from her home by the Jews in the early hours of this morning. The hostage takers drove a dark estate car. Part of the licence plate of this car is C699.'

'What else?'

'Nothing else. We await your orders, sir.'

'Who's *we*?'

'Me and my comrade, sir.'

Aziz looked again at this curiously self-assured, respectful and well-informed youth. What most impressed him was Mo's immediate, unsolicited loyalty. An enormous question mark hung over his abilities as an agent, however. The wrong man in the field could endanger both his daughter's life and his whole business operation.

'Precisely what experience do you have in this aspect of security work?' he asked suddenly.

'Three operations, independently planned and successfully executed, sir,' replied Mo.

'What kind of operations?'

'One assassination, two high-profile property targets destroyed.'

This last piece of information told Aziz exactly who Mo was. He smiled approvingly. Now it would be a simple matter to draw him and his unnamed *comrade* into a cast-iron trap. An exchange of hostages would follow, and everything could return to the way it was before.

But for the first time in more than a decade, this did not strike Aziz as an attractive proposition. Dexter's arrogance had become insufferable. His company outperformed Aziz's in every sector and now he was using Beirut tactics to get his own way. This boy must be good, since he had evaded detection by both the police and Dexter. He had the right experience, the right attitude and the right personal qualities to be an invaluable long-term asset. Besides which, as long as the boy remained loyal, he could be turned over to Dexter whenever that might become expedient.

Mo shifted his weight from one foot to the other then back again, subtly reminding Aziz that he was still standing there. Aziz smiled for a second time. Since he had made his decision, it was time to get down to business.

'What weaponry do you have at your disposal?' he asked.

'Our hands and minds – and a couple of knives, I guess.'

'So – apart from guns, what else do you want from me?'

'Operational leadership, sir.'

'What's your name, son?'

'Mo – Mohammed, sir.'

'Well – ' Aziz paused. 'Sergeant Major. We already have an auspicious name in common. Come with me.'

Mo followed him out of the office, along a corridor and into a lift. Aziz fished out a small brass key and unlocked a compartment under the lift buttons. Inside was another button, which he pushed twice. The doors closed and the lift dropped like a stone.

'Fucking shit,' gasped Mo, as his stomach pressed up against his diaphragm.

Aziz appeared mildly amused, but not in the least concerned. After a short time, the brakes were applied and the lift jolted to a slower pace, then came to a complete stop. The doors slid open and they stepped out into a dark concrete bunker. Aziz patted the wall; rows of striplights flickered across the low ceiling.

The subterranean room was much bigger than Mo had first thought – more like Wembley Arena than a coal cellar. Tall banks of steel shelving, running the length of the bunker, had been constructed at three-feet intervals up to each of the side walls. The shelves at the front were neatly stacked with anonymous brown cardboard boxes. Aziz led him past these to the back wall, then along to the right.

'Here,' said Aziz, disappearing down one of the rows.

He came back out holding two .38 automatic pistols, two spare clips and a box of live ammunition.

'My recommendation,' said Aziz, handing the weapons to Mo, 'is that you never fire these guns. But if you threaten to fire them in a combat situation, then you must be prepared to actually fire them. Otherwise your gesture will be worse than useless. Do you understand?'

'Yes, sir.'

'Good. I never want to see, or hear, of these guns again. Your operation will be in deep cover, understood?'

'Yes, sir.'

'I shall furnish you with the necessary intelligence. We will communicate by means of compact handportables. One moment . . .'

Aziz went along another bank of shelves and returned with a pair of portable phones. He gave one of them to Mo.

'This channel of communication is not secure. You will therefore address me by rank, not by name.'

'Sir?'

'My rank? Colonel. Come, now.'

They paced slowly back to the lift door. Aziz motioned to Mo to conceal the guns. He stuck one pistol in the back of his jeans and the other in the inside pocket of his jacket, then followed Aziz into the lift.

Back at street level, Aziz put a fatherly arm round Mo's shoulders and led him out through reception to the main entrance. They shook hands in silence, then Aziz went back in to inform his committee that they had just been replaced by a teenage boy.

Mo was relieved to see the back of Aziz. The serve-and-obey bullshit had really been starting to get to him. He figured that he'd made a good job of it, though. He had got them some help, some goodwill, and the guns. Wrinklies like Aziz just needed to get off on that old-style establishment rap.

Tayeb was waiting for Mo to get back. He had kind of drifted off to sleep – but he was right there in his room, where he had said he would be. When Mo rang the doorbell, he was up and down the stairs like a shot.

'I've got it!' he shouted at his mother.

His mother sighed, turned around and went back into the kitchen. Tayeb opened the door and high-fived with Mo.

'How d'you make out?'

'Upstairs, man,' said Mo.

He had seen the kitchen door hanging just an inch ajar. His own mother used all the same tricks.

When they got up to Tayeb's room, Mo shut the door and put a tape on. Then he gave Tayeb his gun.

'Shit! Well hard, man!'

'Watch yourself, guy – it's for real.'

'I can see that,' said Tayeb, squinting down the barrel.

'Then don't point it in your own motherfucking face!'

'All right, all right . . .'

Tayeb put the pistol down.

'So, what do we do now?'

Mo took the portable phone out of his jacket and stood it on the bedside table.

'We wait.'

The young computer operator leaned back in his seat, cracked his knuckles, and started picking at one of his blackheads.

'We're in,' he said finally, as if no explanation should have been necessary.

Aziz looked at the single green asterisk flashing in the top left-hand corner of the screen. It didn't tell him anything.

'I want the owner of a dark estate car, licence plate C699.'

The operator typed away as Aziz spoke, then suddenly stopped. He left his fingers poised dramatically over the keyboard.

'Yes?' he asked, after a long silence.

'Yes, what?'

'C699 – what?' yawned the operator.

'That's all there is,' snapped Aziz.

The operator shrugged, tapped in another line of command codes and hit return. The screen went blank for a moment, then flashed up a page of registration numbers paired with names and addresses. The operator scrolled rapidly forward through the list. There were over a thousand entries.

'What now?' he asked, glancing at his watch.

Aziz chose to ignore both the irritating gesture and the impatient tone of his voice.

'Now you cross reference this list of names with the list in file employees-dot-D.'

'I'm not a secretary,' snorted the operator, punching at the keyboard with deliberate, one-finger slowness.

Aziz frowned deeply. He was unimpressed by this spotty youth, who plainly thought he was far too clever to be required to show any respect.

The computer bleeped assertively and produced a single match: Isaac Hamilton.

'Show me that file,' said Aziz.

'OK, I'll *display that record*,' the operator replied.

Aziz ground his teeth, narrowed his eyes and tried to concentrate on the screen. It told him that Isaac had been on Dexter's payroll since at least April 1978. That meant he was part of the old gang, which meant there was a good chance he was using one of the old network of safehouses. It was time to send his newly enlisted commandos on a little reconnaissance mission. He turned to go.

'You finished with me?' asked the operator, standing up and slinging his jacket over his shoulder.

'Just one more thing,' Aziz said icily.

'Yeah?'

'Pick up your P45 on your way out.'

CHAPTER 18

Mo and Tayeb left King's Cross station by the Cheney Road exit. Mo shifted the holdall he was carrying from his left to his right hand and looked at his watch. Three hours, three doors busted open, three long-abandoned, derelict buildings searched. And Aziz always had another *promising location* for them to investigate every time they reported in.

'You take a turn,' he said testily, swinging the heavy canvas bag up into Tayeb's arms.

Tayeb accepted the burden without protest. He was wondering how they were going to play it when they finally hit on the right place – if Mo had a plan. He pushed the holdall up on to his left shoulder and reached around the waistband of his jeans, feeling the butt of the pistol pressed hard into the small of his back. Maybe that would be enough – show them the gun, grab Rashida, and split.

'Coming up on the right,' said Mo.

They followed the same precise drill each time, walking on past the entrance to the target street, with only the most casual glance along it. As they neared the opposite kerb, Tayeb's chest tightened suddenly, nearly bouncing the bag off his shoulder. Partly hidden behind a skip full of junk, was the car that had taken Rashida – he was sure of it. He put the holdall down on the pavement and took a deep breath.

'You see it?' he whispered.

'Uh-huh.'

Mo looked all around them. Aside from the constant rush of traffic up and down the main road, they were alone. He bent down, unzipped the bag and pulled out the portable phone Aziz had issued him with.

'Let's go,' he said.

Tayeb refastened the holdall and followed Mo's cautious progress down the left-hand side of the street. When they drew level with the car, Mo signalled Tayeb to keep watch while he crossed over to check its number plate.

Crouching down between the skip and the back of the Volvo estate, Mo was straight on the phone to Aziz.

'We've got the car, Colonel.'

'Where is it?'

'Spitting distance from our next location – sir.'

'Very good,' said Aziz. 'Proceed with the greatest of care. My daughter's safety is paramount, and she is *your* responsibility. Acknowledge.'

'I've got it – '

'And keep me informed. Out.'

Mo switched the phone to standby, then scrambled to his feet and waved Tayeb over. Together they approached the target building. The only way in was through its inch-thick metal security door.

'How're we gonna get through that?' asked Tayeb.

'There's tools in the bag, dummy.'

'I didn't see no plastic explosives or oxy-er-whatsit cutting gear, man.'

'Shut up and make yourself useful,' said Mo, digging a battery-powered electric drill out of the holdall.

'Doing what?'

'Just get in front of the door, facing it. Now crouch down there.'

Tayeb did as he was told. When he was low enough, Mo stepped over him and sat on his shoulders.

'Now stand up again.'

'Easy to say,' grunted Tayeb.

But with a little effort, he managed to raise them both up to his full height. Mo immediately set to work, boring out the masonry around one of the top set of bolts that were holding the door unit in place. When that one felt loose enough, he moved on to the next. After nearly twenty minutes of intensive drilling, he slid down Tayeb's back and started working along the side bolts.

The persistent whining noise of the drill was worrying Tayeb. He kept on looking up and down the deserted street, then back at the door – expecting an alert enemy force to burst out at any moment.

He thought it might be a good idea to practise drawing his pistol. Every time he grabbed the handle, the sighting lug on the end of the barrel snagged on the waist of his boxer shorts. This made a quick draw at best uncomfortable, at worst impossible. He decided that when the time came to attack, the gun was already going to be in his hand.

'I'm done,' Mo said finally.

He dropped the drill into the canvas bag, then went over to the skip and shoved a pile of plasterboard and plastic piping off into the street. Underneath was a badly stained, slashed-up old mattress. Tayeb watched him curiously.

'Get your ass over here, willya?' called Mo, who was getting tired of doing everything as well as thinking of everything.

Between the two of them, they succeeded in dragging the mattress out of the skip. Tayeb helped Mo position it lengthways in front of the loosened security door, then took a couple of steps back and prepared to cover the entrance. Mo lifted a heavyweight crowbar out of the holdall and set about prising the whole unit away from the wall.

The door creaked and groaned under the strain, then the bolts came popping out from between the bricks, one after the other in rapid succession. A final wrench on the crowbar and the cast-iron slab jumped forward a couple of inches, wavered on its edge for a moment, then fell flat on to the mattress with a dull, metallic thud.

Tayeb stood with his legs apart, holding his pistol with both hands stretched out in front of him. Facing him was a long empty passageway, dimly lit by a string of red bulbs. He nodded to Mo, who gathered up the tool bag, drew his gun and rushed in and along the corridor. It was only then that Tayeb remembered to take his safety catch off.

'You could've fucked up real bad there,' he chided himself as he followed after Mo, covering him for real this time.

They kept on going to the end of the passageway and down the spiral staircase. Mo tried the basement door. To his surprise, the handle turned easily. He put a finger to his lips, edged the door carefully past the frame, then pushed it wide open. They leapt into the room, waving their pistols wildly from side to side, both trying to cover all four corners at once.

Almost straight away, they realised that there was nobody there to shoot. They put up their guns and moved warily around the office, thinking of spyholes and booby traps. Mo edged over to the desk and peered into the monitor. He saw what looked like a cell, with a table and bed ... and buried under the covers, somebody stirring! He looked up at the other door, opposite the one they had come in through. The key was in the lock. He whistled softly to get Tayeb's attention.

'Ten to one, she's on the other side of that door,' he said with a knowing smile.

Tayeb jumped to it, pouncing on the key and throwing open the cell door. He laid his gun on the table, knelt down by the bed and gently turned back the covers.

His head jerked back with disgust, the stench of the dwarf's breath hitting him a split second before the sight of his lumpy grey skin, drooling mouth and watery yellow eyes.

'It's a trap!' shouted Tayeb, grabbing for his pistol.

Isaac saw a vague shadowy movement and heard some distant sounds. A thought emanating from somewhere in the depths of his brain suggested that the self-adminis-tered anaesthetic was beginning to wear off.

In his haste, Tayeb sent his pistol spinning across the table on to the floor. It went off with a loud bang as Mo reached the doorway. A bullet ricocheted off the walls. Mo dropped to the floor; Tayeb vaulted on to the table.

'What the fuck . . .?' Mo gasped, lifting his head to see Tayeb standing unarmed on the table and Isaac lying peacefully in bed.

Tayeb climbed shakily down to the floor, picked up his gun and put the safety catch back on. Mo threw him a withering look, then dragged himself up and on to the bed. He sat astride the dwarf's bulky chest, pinning him down at the shoulders with his knees. Then he pointed his gun at Isaac's left eye.

'Where's the girl?' he asked, putting a gangster slur in his voice.

Isaac thought he heard something about a girl. He felt the weight of a body pressing down on him, and started feeling warmer. *She likes being on top, that's all it was.*

He smiled dreamily and sensed the beginnings of a hard on.

A searing pain shot through his groin. He screamed uncontrollably and his head jumped forward, jabbing his eye on the muzzle of Mo's pistol. An unpleasant awareness of reality was closing in on him as his head flopped back down on to the pillow.

'Get some ice or something,' said Mo. 'And pass me the mobile phone.'

'Yes, master,' said Tayeb, bowing low and tugging an imaginary forelock.

He quickly found the fridge and scraped a big heap of ice out of the freezer compartment on to a plate. On his way back to the cell, he picked up the portable phone and proffered the two items to Mo for his approval.

'We ain't got your girlie yet,' Mo reminded him, fully appreciating the sarcasm in Tayeb's gestures.

He grabbed a handful of ice with his free hand and rubbed it roughly over Isaac's face. Then he snatched the phone off Tayeb and punched in Aziz's number. Isaac spluttered and groaned. Mo forced the barrel of the gun into his mouth, chipping a couple of teeth.

'Fucking shut up!' he yelled, then more quietly, 'Not you, Colonel. I've got a prisoner here. There's no sign of the hostage.'

'Who is your prisoner?'

'I dunno – a butt-ugly dwarf. I've seen him before, he's off on drugs or – '

'The name of your prisoner,' Aziz cut across, 'is Isaac Hamilton. When you have extracted the intelligence you require, kill him.'

'Yes, Sir.'

'Out.'

Mo handed the phone back to Tayeb, then slapped Isaac

round the face. He could see the prisoner's eyes were
beginning to focus. Now was the time to get it out of him,
while his defences were low.

'Where have they taken the girl?' Mo asked.

He spoke very slowly and clearly, and only took the
gun out of Isaac's mouth when he had finished. The dwarf
looked very confused. He tried to turn his head to look
around but Mo slapped it back with the gun barrel,
bruising his cheek. Isaac stared up into Mo's face; his
eyes went moist and blurry.

'They've gone fishing,' he said distantly.

'What the fuck does that mean?' snarled Mo.

But Isaac wasn't sure himself what it meant. It made
him feel very sad, though. His friends had gone fishing
and left him all alone in the children's home. But he
knew that couldn't be right – he was a grown man, it was
the drug combination fucking him up. He couldn't help
being upset, though. Tears sprang from his eyes and
trickled down the sides of his face.

'He's losing it again,' Mo grumbled. 'Get some more of
that ice on him, man.'

Tayeb dumped the rest of the ice over Isaac's head and
sat back down on the table. As the freezing water encir-
cled his skull, Isaac forgot about being unhappy and just
began to feel cold. Mo tried again.

'What have you done with the girl?'

Isaac blinked, and saw a man's face looming over him,
an Arab – no, worse than that – it was one of the two
Arab boys they had been looking for. And he had a gun.
He tried desperately to get his brain moving, to fix on
some sort of strategy. But Mo had seen full consciousness
return to his prisoner's eyes.

'Tell me where the girl is,' he said quietly, 'or I'll kill
you.'

'You'll kill me anyway,' whined Isaac, hoping Mo would offer some arrangement to guarantee his safety if he talked.

'Fetch the drill, man,' Mo said calmly.

Tayeb stared at him in disbelief, not moving a muscle.

'Do it!'

Mo raised his voice this time. He turned his head towards Tayeb and shot him a threatening glance. Tayeb fetched the drill. Mo selected the lowest speed and started the motor. The little metal bit whirred smoothly round in its socket.

'I'm gonna start with your left eye,' said Mo, 'seeing as how it's already kinda fucked up.'

'No, wait, stop!' shrieked Isaac.

He tried to squirm out from under Mo, but there was no power in his drugged-out limbs. Mo held back with the drill, but kept it running just a few inches from Isaac's face.

'OK, OK,' Isaac said weakly. 'If I tell you, you'll let me go – that's the deal, right?'

Mo nodded once, down and up.

'How do I know you'll keep your side?'

'You've gotta trust me.'

Isaac looked unconvinced.

'I've gotta trust *you*. You might tell me a lie,' Mo said menacingly.

'No, no – I'll tell the truth,' Isaac promised.

'Let's hear it, then.'

'Put the drill away first.'

Mo shrugged, turned off the motor and held the drill out at arm's length. Tayeb's hands trembled as he took it back from him.

'She's somewhere along the Grand Union Canal,' Isaac volunteered.

'The motherfucker's drowned her!' shouted Tayeb, leaping forward with the drill still in his hand.

'On a barge! On a barge!' squealed Isaac.

Mo stuck out an arm to hold Tayeb back, but his anger had vanished the moment he knew that Rashida was still alive.

'It's a long canal,' Mo observed.

'Between here and the Thames.'

'Where're they taking her – in the end?'

Isaac wasn't sure how to reply. Trying to stall them promised to be a grotesquely damaging experience, but coughing up the full story could well prove fatal. A sickly feeling of terror washed over him as he realised that his only real hope for survival was a radical change in circumstances. And that meant holding out for as long as he possibly could.

'I don't know,' he lied feebly.

'You're lying,' sighed Mo, reaching for the drill.

CHAPTER 19

Emmy settled into the back of his taxi, put on his spectacles and opened up a pocket-size book of crossword puzzles. He was soon engrossed in challenge number eighty-nine.

As the cab turned into King's Cross station, he glanced up at the rooftop clock: half past two in the morning. He had meant to leave the casino earlier, but even millionaires don't pass up a winning streak on the craps table. Anyway, guarding prisoners was a physical job – and he was paid for using his brain, not his body.

He walked the short distance up Cheney Road from the station to the safe-house. As he approached the building itself, he was surprised to see the door wide open. Issac's car was still parked outside, so he hadn't gone anywhere in a hurry. Emmy wondered if he'd had to call an ambulance, but he doubted it: too many awkward questions.

A few yards further on, he was close enough to see that the door wasn't so much open as completely dismantled and lying on the pavement. A cursory analysis of the facts led Emmy to conclude that something had gone wrong. He stepped silently through the doorway and crept along the corridor to the top of the stairs.

Pausing there momentarily, he listened out for any telltale sounds from the basement. The absolute silence of the place was reassuring, if somewhat unnerving.

Feeling decidedly unhappy about the absence of any

alternative, Emmy slowly descended the first few steps. Then it suddenly occurred to him that he *did* have an alternative: running away.

He lost no time in putting this great new plan into effect, turning swiftly about face and charging back up the stairs. As he touched the top step, the hand-stitched leather soles of his new brogues skidded away from under him and he slid bumping and rolling all the way down to the basement floor.

At first, Emmy didn't bother opening his eyes. He wasn't the type to refuse a blindfold when facing the firing squad. However, after a count of ten, when still nothing terrible had happened to him, he summoned up the courage to take a look. The office was as devoid of human presence as the corridor and stairwell had been.

Very shakily, he picked himself up. His shoes were scuffed, his suit was torn and his hands were flecked with tiny grazes. His left cheek had been the first part of his body to make contact with the office carpet, and it was swelling up into an unsightly and painful blister.

Emmy felt convinced that he was the victim of a deeply unjust destiny. But once he had taken a few stiff paces to the cell door, he realised just how lucky a person he was.

Isaac's face was a mass of purple-edged scars and bruises. The small patches of undamaged skin were a sickly blend of grey and yellow. His left eye had disappeared into a socket full of congealed blood, leaving his right eye staring blankly up at the ceiling. An unpleasant odour of contaminated dead meat was just beginning to rise off the corpse.

Emmy felt his stomach start to turn. He slammed the door on Isaac's remains and staggered over to the desk. Sitting down, he was offered a different angle on the body, courtesy of the closed-circuit monitor.

As he leaned forward to switch it off, the telephone rang. For a moment Emmy thought he might have become an unwitting contestant in a hidden-camera TV show. The host would be calling now to tell him that it had all been a hilarious practical joke.

But he had to concede that this was an exceptionally unlikely scenario. The smell, especially, would have been very difficult to fake. He stopped trying to think and picked up the phone.

'Hello?'

'Who is that?' the caller demanded.

'Who wants to know?' Emmy coyly inquired.

'Is Isaac there?'

'Erm – well, he can't come to the phone right now – '

'This is Mr Dexter!'

'Oh, I'm sorry – excuse me, Mr Dexter, sir – Emmanuel speaking,' flannelled Emmy.

'What the bloody hell is going on?' Dexter thundered.

Emmy hesitated; he was far from convinced that he could provide a satisfactory answer to *that* particular question.

'Could you be a bit more precise?' he ventured.

There was a short, baffled silence at the other end of the line, then Dexter's voice came blaring through at maximum volume.

'Go and get Isaac!' he commanded.

'He's dead!' Emmy shouted back, inadvertently raising his own voice to match Dexter's.

'What?'

'Isaac has been killed.'

'What about the hostage – and your colleagues?'

'I don't know,' Emmy confessed.

'Stay on the line.'

Dexter laid down the receiver and rubbed his hands

over his face. Being up this late made him depressingly aware of how old he had become. This latest killing must have been Aziz's doing: he had the motive and he probably knew about the safe-house. He didn't know about the new place, though – Dexter was sure of that. Since only Isaac appeared to be dead and he had heard nothing from the others, it was a pretty safe bet that the hostage was being moved according to plan.

He smiled grimly. One casualty, but he still controlled the game. There was just one thing which didn't quite make sense. Why kill Isaac if the hostage was no longer with him? He snatched up the phone.

'How was Isaac killed?'

'It's a little hard to tell,' said Emmy. 'Multiple cuts and contusions, a possible bullet wound – '

'Does he appear to have been tortured?'

'I would say it's a distinct possibility.'

Which meant that the new place of safety was probably no more secure than the old one. The hostage would have to be moved again as soon they got her there, Dexter decided. And he would have to get this halfwit to organise it.

'Emmanuel, I have a little job for you . . .'

CHAPTER 20

'Are you a real princess?' asked Rachel.

Rashida looked curiously at her latest jailer. A woman half her size was probably half her strength and – if the midget's opening question was anything to go by – she was hardly a power-brain either. Things were looking up.

'No I'm not,' she answered, sticking to the truth for the time being.

'Oh,' said Rachel, clearly disappointed. 'It's just I never met a *real* princess.'

Rashida sighed inwardly. As she tried to think of a fresh opener for conversation, she felt the barge drift to a stop. A moment later, she heard the sound of rushing water. Another lock, and they always went down. This didn't tell her anything about where they were but, irritatingly enough, she was sure that it should have done. Downriver meant down to the sea, but did the same reasoning apply to canals? Was she bound for a slow boat over the ocean and far away to the Land of the Little People?

Realising that these speculations were getting her nowhere, Rashida turned her attention back to Rachel. It was too late now to assert any royal ancestry, but there had to be some way of winning the midget over.

'Actually, I'm a variety artiste,' she said grandly, trying to sound important and celebrated.

'Me too,' Rachel enthused, looking up from her rolling mat. 'I'm a stripper – what do you do?'

'I'm a *chanteuse*,' Rashida replied, stuck in grand mode and more than a little boggled by the thought of Rachel undressing in front of a paying audience.

'Is that some kind of speciality act?' Rachel asked innocently, as she eased the roach into the end of her joint.

'I mean, I'm a singer,' Rashida translated.

She was beginning to hope that where nobility and celebrity had failed her, the common bond of life on the stage might succeed. Regretting the pretentiousness of her earlier declarations, she assembled her reserve forces of vapid, girlish charm and tried again.

'It must be really interesting being a stripper,' she said with a bland smile.

'Mm-mm,' Rachel confirmed, drawing heavily on the spliff.

There was a necessary lull in the conversation while she held the smoke down. She carried on talking as she exhaled.

'Yeah, it's like – well, I do it with my husband. Not *it*,' she giggled, 'not on stage, anyway. I mean, you know, we do a routine together . . .'

She started giggling again and had to take another deep drag to stifle it.

'You're both strippers in the same act?' Rashida suggested.

'Yeah . . . D'you want any of this?'

Rachel waved the joint in her general direction. Rashida shook her head and coughed lightly.

'It's a bit stuffy down here,' she remarked. 'It's a pity there aren't any windows to open.'

'Oh, no – it's just as well,' said Rachel, 'or all the water would come in.'

'Maybe you could open that hatch,' Rashida went on, her eyes fixed on the only escape route from the hold.

'I can't,' said Rachel, after a long pause.

'Why not?'

'It's locked from the outside, see?'

She clamped the joint firmly between her teeth, went over to the ladder under the hatch, and hauled herself up to the fourth rung. Wedging her knees in for balance, she stretched up and rattled it as hard as she could.

The hatch stayed shut but Rachel's knees slipped out from under the fifth rung of the ladder. The half-smoked joint torpedoed out of her mouth as she landed flat on the floor of the hold, completely winded.

Leon was on the tiller when he heard a rattling from below, followed by a loud thump which sent the barge wobbling off towards the left bank. He dragged on the handle to steer it back towards the middle of the canal. The barge responded slowly, levelling up just in time to scrape its whole length noisily along the edge of the tow-path. Leon turned off the motor and called out to Jerry and Rabin, who had settled themselves somewhere in front.

'Hey! Someone has to check the hold, while someone else checks the side for damage!'

'You do it!' Rabin shouted back.

He and Jerry were enjoying the wonderfully sweaty, if slightly claustrophobic, experience of making love under a heavy, rubberised tarpaulin. The wild pitch and toss of the last manoeuvre had only served to reinforce their fantasy of illicit passion on the high seas.

Leon figured that since they weren't sinking the side of the barge was probably all right. He went over to the hatch to the hold and stamped on it three times.

'You all right down there?' he shouted.

Rashida had stayed where she was, unable to decide whether to try to help the fallen midget or attempt to turn the situation to her own advantage. Anyway, Rachel was starting to get her breath back now. She called up between little shallow gasps.

'I – fell – down!'

'Are you OK now?' Leon shouted back.

An idea came to Rashida. She jumped to her feet and started yelling as loud as she could.

'Fire! Fire!'

Now Leon was thoroughly confused. He was going to have to see for himself what was really happening. He slid the bolts back as quietly as possible, eased the hatch open a crack and peeped in.

Rashida suddenly realised what had given her that terribly clever idea. Rachel's joint had landed on a pile of oily rags, which were now giving off worryingly large clouds of acrid black smoke. Seeing Leon's face appear over the top of the ladder, she started yelling again, a new note of genuine hysteria in her voice.

Leon smelled the smoke, heard the cries and saw Rashida waving her arms about like a crazy woman. It occurred to him that she might have started the fire deliberately after Rachel's fall, but right now that was beside the point. He grabbed a fire extinguisher from next to the engine housing and hurried down the ladder into the hold.

The moment he turned the extinguisher on the burning rags, Rashida made a dash for the hatch. But Leon had been expecting this. He whipped around, spraying waves of slippery foam over the floor. Rashida skidded and fell, bruising her knees. Trying to ignore the pain, she slithered over to the bottom of the ladder.

Leon finished putting the fire out. He turned to see Rashida getting her first firm grip on the ladder and Rachel lying flat on her back, in grave danger of being drowned by the rising tide of extinguisher foam.

'Jerry! Rabin! She's escaping!' he screamed at the top of his voice, then bent down and gently cupped his hands under Rachel's head, lifting her face out of danger.

'I'd better see what's happening,' sighed Jerry, kissing Rabin on the tip of his nose.

He gathered a length of tarpaulin around his waist and stood up to look. At the other end of the barge, Rashida's head and shoulders were struggling out through the hatch. Jerry dived back down and grabbed Rabin by the arm.

'Quick, she's getting away!'

'All right, all right,' grumbled Rabin, trying to find his underwear.

'There's no time for modesty, darling,' said Jerry, throwing off the tarpaulin.

A policeman on night patrol in Victoria Park saw two naked boys scrambling along either side of a barge to the rear, where they started having a heated argument with their mother. He remembered what his old sergeant used to call the three Ds: Don't get involved in Domestic Disputes.

'Fucking gippo boat-people,' he muttered under his breath.

It was nearly three in the morning, the dead of night, and they were disturbing the peace, not wearing life jackets, probably moored illegally – he could have sworn one of the lads just slapped his mother right across the face.

'She brought them up like that – she's only herself to blame,' he decided, and continued on his beat.

Jerry and Rabin succeeded in shoving Rashida back down into the hold. She landed heavily on her backside, only slightly cushioned by the sea of foam. Rachel sat up suddenly.

'You're all right!' Leon shouted accusingly.

'Yeah – I think so,' Rachel admitted.

Jerry and Rabin jumped down after Rashida and pinned her arms behind her back. Leon and Rachel stared at them.

'Do you realise you're both stark, bollock naked?' asked Leon.

'How're we meant to dress for a bubble bath?' Jerry retorted, kicking a dollop of foam in his face.

Rachel got a fit of the giggles.

'What're we gonna do with the princess?' Rabin cut in, tightening his grip on Rashida's right arm.

'I don't know,' said Leon.

'Isaac put you in charge, sweetness,' Rachel reminded him, between giggles.

'He was delirious.'

Rashida was bruised all over and feeling thoroughly defeated. Surely her father would have paid the ransom or whatever it was by now, she thought. Then she remembered Tayeb. But she still couldn't see any way of them knowing about him and her – unless they found him in her flat. And then, why take her? She felt that if there was one thing she had succeeded in doing, it was to make herself more trouble than she was worth.

'The most important thing,' said Leon, 'is to get moving again. We're way behind schedule.'

'That isn't my fault,' Rachel said quietly.

Rabin, Jerry and Leon stared at her in complete disbelief.

'Oh, yes it is!' they burst out in unison.

CHAPTER 21

Trafalgar Square was under occupation by the four tribes of homeward-bound clubbers. Mo and Tayeb's night bus terminated just short of westbound territory, the natives of which displayed more fun fur, designer rubber and radical piercings on their bodies than all the east, north and south dwelling party people put together.

Turning their backs on the free fashion show, the two youths hurried off down Northumberland Avenue. Mo knew that the bulky holdall would attract the attention of any loitering policemen. Planting a bullet in one or two stop-and-search fascists didn't bother him, but starting like that meant finishing with a flying squad shoot-out.

'D'you think he was telling the truth?' asked Tayeb, finally voicing the concern which had kept them in mutual silence since leaving King's Cross.

'We ain't got nothing else to go on,' said Mo.

'Yeah – it's just . . .'

'What?'

Like a kid brother tagging along after him, questioning everything he did, Tayeb was getting on Mo's nerves.

'Well, if you hadn't killed him – '

'That freakoid?' Mo spat. 'Listen man, if that piece of shit was still alive, he'd have a whole army out there waiting for us. You don't understand anything.'

Mo couldn't be bothered to argue on. As far as he was concerned, he had been hired by Aziz to get his daughter

back. Tayeb could go and sort out his love life later on –
along with the rest of his problems.

As they turned down Victoria Embankment, a black
cab drew up opposite the tube station. Emmy jumped out
on to the pavement and fished through his wallet for a
suitably small denomination note. The smallest he could
find was a twenty. He stood up on tiptoe and passed it
through the window to the driver – which was when he
saw the two Arabs on the other side of the street.

Recognising Tayeb at once, Emmy snatched the bank-
note away and dived back into the taxi.

'Would you take me once more round the block?' he
asked in a tremulous voice. 'It's such a fine evening.'

The cabbie had been eyeing the exciting bulge in
Emmy's wallet, and was only too happy to oblige.

Mo saw the taxi stop, wait and drive away again, but
nobody got in or out, and he didn't see any passenger in
the back when it passed by. It was probably just a
coincidence, but the cab had stopped right in front of
Charing Cross Pier – which was where Isaac had told
them to go.

'You see that?' he asked Tayeb.

'See what?'

Mo's anger burst up to the surface. He dumped the bag
on the ground and smacked Tayeb hard across the face
with the flat of his hand. Tears of pain and bewilderment
clouded Tayeb's eyes, but he defiantly kept them from
falling.

'Pay attention,' Mo suggested coldly.

He set off across the road towards the pier, leaving
Tayeb to carry the bag. As soon as Mo's back was turned,
Tayeb wiped his eyes on the sleeve of his jacket. He had
thought they were meant to be friends – but that was
before Mo started playing the big-shot gang leader.

For the time being, however, he had little choice but to go along with it, bullshit and all. With this thought, his feelings of hurt and humiliation turned to bitterness. He snatched up the holdall and followed after Mo, resolving never to see him again after they had rescued Rashida.

While he was waiting for Tayeb to catch up, Mo inspected the covered entrance to the pier. The door was securely locked, but it looked like an easy climb over the top and down to the quayside. The only real worry was that they would be highly visible from all sides as long as they stayed on the roof.

'All right?' he asked pleasantly, as Tayeb lumbered up with the holdall.

Tayeb was dumbfounded. Mo was acting like nothing had happened, as if they hadn't just permanently fallen out.

'You give me a leg up,' Mo said. 'Then pass me the bag and I'll pull you up after – OK?'

The sloping roof was coated with a kind of weatherproof grit, which provided a firm grip for their trainers. And a little way along on the other side was a ladder leading down to the water's edge. Everything seemed perfect, until Mo heard the distinctive rumble of a black cab approaching along the embankment.

'Get down!' he hissed.

They scrambled over to the side of the roof facing away from the road and flattened themselves against it. The taxi driver saw nothing out of the ordinary – but Emmy did. He was quite sure what the Arabs were up to now, he just wasn't sure what to do about it.

'I *am* enjoying myself,' he said to the driver. 'Let's do another tour.'

'Twenty-six pounds on the clock, guv,' the cabbie felt obliged to mention.

Emmy peeled off a fifty-pound note and stuck it in the glass partition behind the driver's right ear.

'Let me know when we've used that up,' he said warmly.

Mo listened carefully as the taxi rattled past and off into the distance. It hadn't stopped, so it was probably another coincidence – there were hundreds if not thousands of them working the streets of London.

'Let's go!' he commanded.

They scurried along to the ladder and down on to the floating landing platform. Moored there was a double-decker pleasure cruiser, which had been decorated with plywood extensions to look a little like a Mississippi steamboat.

Of considerably more interest to Mo and Tayeb, some twenty yards out towards the middle of the Thames, was their target vessel. The massive commercial dredger was anchored off Hungerford Bridge, as Isaac had promised. He had also said that it was accessible from the pier, but had failed to point out that they would have to fly, swim or walk on water to reach it.

Mo took another look at the pleasure boat. They could probably break into it easily enough, but he wouldn't have the faintest idea how to start the engine, let alone drive the thing. And it was hardly an inconspicuous mode of transport for what was meant to be a sneak attack.

He paced the length of the gently bobbing platform, trying to figure out how to get across. Swimming was out of the question; they would have to leave the tool bag behind and they had no way of keeping their guns dry. He reached the end of the quay and turned back. Maybe they could stake it out from here – but that wouldn't help them get Rashida away.

An intense feeling of exhaustion crept over him,

making his whole body go heavy and stiff. As he rolled his head back to ease the tension in his neck, his eyes lighted on a tiny life raft, hanging off the back of the pleasure boat.

Hopelessly inadequate as it was for the rescue of a hundred or more stricken pleasure trippers, it appeared ideally suited to the rescue of a single hostage. Mo whistled softly, which brought Tayeb running over.

Their progress in getting the life raft off the back of the boat and into the water was closely followed by Emmy. He had asked the driver to stop by Cleopatra's Needle so that he could sit back and admire the view.

As Mo and Tayeb struck out towards the dredger, Emmy finally decided on the required course of action. The others would be coming upriver from the east and they had to be warned, stopped and turned back before they sailed into whatever trap was being laid for them.

He leaned forward and tapped on the glass.

'Take me to the middle of Waterloo Bridge and leave me there,' he told the driver.

CHAPTER 22

Leon steered the barge through Limehouse Basin, past the sleeping blocks of pristine executive flats and out on to the Thames. This was the only really dodgy leg of the journey, since they hadn't had time to assemble the stack of official paperwork required for legitimate access to the river.

Down in the hold, Jerry and Rabin were completing the mopping-up operations, only slightly hindered by Rachel's assistance. Rashida had curled up and gone to sleep on top of the wooden boiler casing, which was hard and uncomfortable but warm and dry too. She was jolted awake again, after what felt like only a minute, by a shriek of raucous laughter.

'You've missed a bit, boys!' Rachel cackled, pointing to a small puddle of water in the back left-hand corner.

'I did there first,' grumbled Jerry, advancing on it with his mop.

As he got closer, the puddle seemed to grow. And the water wasn't all foamy, like the rest of it had been. He was about to say something when he heard a muffled splintering sound. A thin jet of water sprayed up from the middle of the ever-widening puddle.

'Man the pumps!' he shouted.

'What pumps?' Rabin shouted back, already banging urgently on the hatch.

Leon flipped back the bolts with the toe of his shoe. Rabin flung open the hatch and clambered up on deck.

'What is it now?' asked Leon, trying not to lose his patience.

'Tell you what,' said Rabin, annoyed by the tone of his voice, 'I'll steer and you go see for yourself, all right?'

He wrestled the tiller away from Leon and gave him a helpful shove towards the entrance to the hold. With an air of selfless martyrdom, Leon knelt by the hatch and poked his head down below.

Water was spurting in through a nasty crack in the port bows, giving considerable cause for alarm. He watched as Jerry frantically mopped at the floor then turned to pursue his plastic bucket, which was floating off to the other end of the hold. Rachel had joined Rashida on top of the boiler and they both looked thoroughly amused, if a little apprehensive. Leon realised, rather too late, that he should have checked for damage after their collision with the tow path.

'All hands on deck!' he called down.

They were less than half an hour from Charing Cross, so Leon figured they should keep going at full speed, while baling out the hold as best they could. As long as they got there before the barge sunk, everything would be all right.

Mo and Tayeb prowled around the dredger, searching for the enemy. Apart from the huge, mud-filled tank which occupied the whole central portion of the vessel, there were very few places to look. The control house was unmanned, the narrow decks were clear and the small storage hold was empty. Either they had been told the wrong place or, with a bit of luck, they had got there first.

Mo decided that the best plan would be to lie low until Rashida and her captors were on board. That would make it harder for them to just bundle her back on the barge and take off. It would also give him and Tayeb a chance to see what sort of force they were going to be dealing with, at least a couple of seconds before they actually had to deal with it.

Tayeb had fallen asleep in a chair by the time Mo finished his final patrol and returned to the control house. He considered waking him, but thought it better to let him rest before the coming battle.

As he settled down to keep watch, Mo started wondering where the kidnappers were. It would be dawn in an hour or so; surely they weren't planning to move their hostage in daylight. He wanted the cover of maximum darkness for *his* operation. And he could do without a crowd of early morning commuters to witness it all from Hungerford Bridge.

Emmy was equally concerned by the non-arrival of the barge. Perched on top of the railings running along the eastern edge of Waterloo Bridge, he scanned the river ahead for any light or sign of movement that could be it.

'Be careful, sir.'

Emmy turned his head in the direction of the voice. A plump, bearded policeman stood about ten feet away, his arms stretched out as if he was holding something very fragile in front of him.

'Why don't you come down over this side for a moment, sir,' the policeman suggested, in a studiously polite and friendly manner.

'I'm quite happy where I am, thank you, officer,' Emmy replied, turning back to watch for the barge.

The policeman felt pleased with himself. He had identified the would-be suicide, approached him in textbook fashion, and had already succeeded in opening a line of communication.

'Would you mind if I came and joined you there, sir?'

'I'd rather you went away,' Emmy said frankly.

That sounded like a classic danger sign to the policeman.

'I'll stay here then, shall I?' he proposed.

Just then, Emmy saw the barge emerge from under Blackfriars Bridge. How on earth was he going to get rid of Porky Pig . . .? Then he realised he didn't have to. Why shouldn't he wave at a passing boat? The policeman thought he was cracked anyway, judging by the way he was talking to him. In fact, if the others saw the uniform nearby, they would know straight away that something was wrong.

As the barge chugged closer, Emmy started to wave – gently at first, so as not to alarm the policeman.

Leon, however, was only looking in two directions: straight ahead and down through the hatch. Jerry stood up to his chest in water, hoisting bucket after bucket up to Rabin, who was slinging them out and passing them back as fast as he could. Rachel and Rashida were standing on the boiler unit now, the water lapping around their ankles.

The barge was almost under Emmy's feet. He saw Leon steering it but however hard he waved he couldn't seem to get his attention. He could hardly call Leon's name with the policeman there, but he had to do something.

'Ahoy there!' he shouted.

'Fuck off,' muttered Leon, without troubling to look up at whatever drunk or lunatic had taken it upon themselves to guard the bridge.

As the barge slipped through the central arch, Emmy whipped around and ran across the road. The policeman raced after him as he leapt up on to the western railings and wavered there, fighting to keep his balance.

The policeman saw a tortured soul, finally unsure of his resolution to end it all, and made a lunging grab for him. Emmy reached out a hand to his aspiring saviour, lost his balance completely and plunged over the edge.

Leon heard a loud splash directly behind him but when he turned to look he saw nothing but ripples. He didn't feel any sympathy for the loud-mouthed drunk, if *that* was what had fallen in.

Mo woke up just in time to see the barge drawing alongside the dredger. He couldn't believe that he had gone to sleep. The sight of Tayeb still snoring away in the chair next to him made him feel all the more annoyed. He shook him roughly by the shoulder.

'Whassup, man?' mumbled Tayeb.

'They're here,' said Mo.

'Who's where?'

There was no time to waste. Mo grabbed hold of Tayeb's chair and tipped him out.

'Your girlie and the freakoid's playmates,' he hissed.

Tayeb woke up fast. He stretched out on the floor, rolled on to his side and drew his pistol.

'They're coming aboard now,' Mo reported from the window.

Rabin jumped across first with the mooring rope. As he tied up the barge, Leon and Jerry dragged Rachel screaming into the deep pool in the hold. They got her to the ladder, pushed her up on deck and went back for Rashida – who was already wading calmly across, the water rising to only just above her waist.

Mo and Tayeb watched from the shadows of the control house as the three other midgets hopped on to the dredger. Finally, Rashida emerged from the hatch and stepped across.

The second he saw her face, Tayeb made a break for the door. Mo caught hold of the back of his jacket, hauling him out of sight as the door swung open and banged noisily against the outer wall.

The boarding party looked up at the control house and watched the door swing gently back and forth until it came to rest. There was no wind and only the smallest of waves lapping the dredger's hull.

'Do you think it's haunted?' whispered Rachel, not wanting to disturb the spirits.

A fearsome rushing, bubbling sound erupted behind them. Rachel turned with the others to face the vengeful phantom, seeing instead the last traces of their barge disappearing beneath the water's surface.

As the barge sunk deeper, it dragged heavily on the mooring rope, causing the dredger to list awkwardly to one side. The rope creaked and groaned under the strain, then finally snapped. With a sudden heave, the dredger righted itself and the control house door banged shut again.

'That explains that,' snorted Rabin.

The hold was directly underneath the control house, but there was no internal route between them. Mo and Tayeb heard the muffled echo of voices and footsteps from below, before the door closed on the new arrivals with a hollow clang.

Now the hostage takers had cornered themselves, Mo decided it was time to move in. He eased open the control house door and waved Tayeb out on to the steps. Holding their pistols in front of them, they commenced a painstakingly noiseless descent.

'How long are we supposed to stay here?' Jerry asked pointedly.

The hold was cramped, unfurnished and distinctly

chilly. There were no toilet or cooking facilities and only a single dim bulb for illumination.

'There's no TV,' Rachel whined despairingly.

'First, I have to call Dexter,' said Leon, ignoring both of them. 'Isaac said there's a short-wave radio in the control house, so that's where I'm going. The rest of you keep an eye on the princess.'

'She isn't a real princess,' sniffed Rachel.

'I don't give a fuck,' Leon retorted, as he walked out on deck.

Mo timed the blow to perfection. The crack of his pistol butt on Leon's skull was completely masked by the bang of the door slamming behind him. Tayeb pulled the unconscious midget clear of the doorway.

'What now?' he whispered.

'Hold this,' said Mo, handing him his gun.

He quickly frisked Leon and discovered that he was unarmed. If the others were as defenceless as this, it was going to be laughably easy. But it would only take one of them holding a knife at Rashida's throat to render their superior firepower completely impotent. Maybe that was a risk they were just going to have to take. Dawn was approaching and time was running out.

Mo also considered the danger of Leon regaining consciousness and launching a rear attack. It seemed like a small risk, but one that might as well be avoided. He slung the midget across his shoulders, then walked up to the central tank and launched him over the railings.

Leon hit the mud with a loud plop and the quieter, crunching sound of his neck breaking on impact. Mo watched with satisfaction as the midget's body was sucked under the surface, the mud smoothing itself over to conceal the evidence.

Tayeb was unable to see the need for this latest murder,

but they were too near their ultimate goal for him to criticise Mo's strategy now.

Mo took his pistol back from Tayeb and seized the door handle.

'Cover me – we're going in,' he whispered.

He pushed the handle down as far as it would go, then pulled open the door with a lightning flick of the wrist.

The midgets looked up, eager for Leon's news.

'Hit the deck! Face down – all of you!' Mo shouted, pointing his gun first at Jerry, then Rabin.

'Not you, Rashida!' called Tayeb, coming up from the rear.

As the three midgets flattened themselves on the floor, Rashida stood up and smiled. Tayeb held out an arm to her. She walked past his tough-looking companion into Tayeb's embrace, kissing him warmly on the lips.

'Let's get out of here,' she sighed, resting her head on his chest.

'Not yet,' Mo snapped, keeping his pistol trained over the heads of his prisoners. 'Take her up to the control house, then bring me the mobile phone.'

Rashida looked questioningly at Tayeb, who nodded quickly then led her out on to the steps. She wanted to know who the other boy was, how they had found her and why she had been kidnapped in the first place. As they went into the control house, she decided to limit herself to one simple question for now.

'Who's he going to call?'

Tayeb looked at her uncertainly. He knew she was not going to like the answer. It would take for ever to explain the ins and outs of their involvement with Aziz. But suddenly the whole situation became clear to him.

'He used to be my friend,' said Tayeb. 'Now he works for your father.'

Rashida heard in his voice the loss of betrayal, of having been betrayed by his friend, and saw in his eyes his fear of losing her too. She wrapped her arms around him and held him close. Then they kissed.

'I've gotta get the phone,' Tayeb mumbled regretfully.

Rashida nodded and let him go and hunt through the holdall for it. When he had found it, he went back over and kissed her again.

Mo was getting impatient. He told his prisoners to stand up and face the wall, as much to pass the time as for any other reason. They had just completed this drill when Tayeb reappeared with the phone.

'About fucking time,' said Mo, snatching it off him.

He cradled the phone in the palm of his left hand and dialled Aziz's number with his thumb, keeping the gun in his right hand pointing at the midgets' backs. While he was waiting to be connected, he glanced around to see Tayeb loitering shiftily in the doorway.

'All right – go on back to your girlie,' Mo said, dismissing him with a shake of his head.

'Good morning, Colonel,' he continued into the phone, as Tayeb hurried back up to the control house.

'Good morning, Sergeant Major,' Aziz replied. 'What do you have to report?'

'I've got your hostage back and I've got three prisoners here – they're all midgets.'

'The hostage – is she unharmed?'

'Yeah, she's fine. I had to bump one of the midgets, though . . .'

Rachel had been wondering where Leon had got to. At first she had imagined him safely up in the control house, calling for help. But when the other Arab came back without him, she had begun to get scared. And now she knew he was dead. Screaming insanely, Rachel sprang at the murderer.

Mo stopped her with a bullet in the chest, then shot her a second time through the head, just to make sure. Jerry and Rabin started to look round but a third shot into the wall above them convinced them to stay where they were.

'Sorry about that, sir,' Mo said impassively. 'It's two dead and two prisoners.'

'Very good,' said Aziz. 'Kill the other two, then bring me the hostage.'

CHAPTER 23

The fat, bearded constable watched sadly from the bridge, as his two colleagues lifted Emmy's body from the water and laid it out on the deck of the police launch. He put his helmet back on, gave a stiff salute, and marched off to the station to fill in his report.

'Do you think he drowned, or was he dead when he hit the water?' the young constable asked his sergeant.

'A tenner says he drowned.'

'How can you tell?'

'At the autopsy – if he's got water in his lungs, he drowned,' the sergeant explained.

'I mean, how can you be sure, just by looking at him?'

'I'm not sure.'

'But, then – '

'Jesus wept!' yelled the sergeant. 'It's a bet – I'm only trying to put a bit of interest in the bloody job – '

The sharp crack of a gunshot, followed by two more at intervals of less than a second, put an end to further discussion. The sergeant radioed in for armed support and began to manoeuvre the launch cautiously up along the south bank. Echoes off the river walls and tall buildings above them made it impossible to pinpoint the exact source of fire, but he was pretty sure that it was upriver and their side of Hungerford Bridge.

Mo switched the portable phone to standby and squeezed off two more rounds: one for Jerry, one for

Rabin. The midgets crumpled, trailing shadowy streaks of blood down the wall.

Now the sergeant was certain. The last two shots, at least, had come from the dredger.

Tayeb watched anxiously from the control house as the police launch circled round and came to a stop, ten yards off their starboard bows. He ducked away from the window and turned to Rashida.

'What the fuck's he playing at?'

'I presume he's just shot them all,' she said numbly.

Tayeb counted on his fingers.

'And then some,' he concluded.

Rashida grimaced, then suppressed a shudder as Mo bounded into the room. She knew he was only carrying out orders, but that made him every bit as terrible as her father. Tayeb sensed the atmosphere and moved quickly to avert a dangerous row.

'Look, man,' he said, leading Mo over to the window.

Mo looked down at the stationary patrol boat. They must have heard the shooting, so why didn't they move in? He guessed they were waiting for reinforcements. And they would have to do that because – like any other bobby on the beat – they didn't carry guns.

'Very good,' he said.

Tayeb stared at him incredulously.

'You reckon?'

'If you do what I tell you,' said Mo.

The sergeant watched through his field glasses as Rashida and Tayeb came down from the control house on to the starboard deck. They had their hands folded on top of their heads. Mo followed, holding his pistol trained on their backs.

'Bring your boat over here,' Mo shouted across, 'or I'll kill the hostages!'

The sergeant could see no alternative. He radioed in a brief report of the developing situation, as he manoeuvred the launch slowly alongside the dredger. The young constable looked like he would sooner have left the hostages to their fate.

'Which one of you's gonna drive?' Mo asked the policemen, as the three of them clambered aboard.

'You do it,' the sergeant told the constable. That way, he would have more freedom to either defuse or take control of the situation.

'That's fine,' said Mo.

He stepped forward and shot the sergeant clean through the back of his head. A shower of sinuous, bloody scraps – all that was left of the sergeant's face – spattered across the constable's fluorescent windcheater.

'Let's go,' Mo said calmly, sticking the muzzle of his pistol in between the constable's shoulder blades.

The policeman thought he was going to faint but, to his great disappointment, he remained fully conscious. Trembling all over, he slammed the launch into motion.

As they sped away under Westminster Bridge, past the Houses of Parliament, a police helicopter hurtled overhead. The radio on the boat, which had been repeatedly requesting any form of acknowledgement, crackled and clicked.

'Please stop the boat and give yourself up,' said a new, distinctly middle-class voice. 'Any political grievances you may have will be communicated to the appropriate authority.'

Mo grinned. He wondered what a real international terrorist would have made of this very English approach. Switching the gun to his left hand, he reached past the constable and unhooked the receiver.

'Tell them if they don't get rid of the chopper, I'll shoot you.'

The constable had every reason to believe Mo's threat, and so made a convincingly fearful plea for his colleagues to abandon the chase. As the launch passed under Battersea Bridge, the helicopter executed a high, banking turn and hovered away to the east.

'Easy,' Mo smiled.

Tayeb and Rashida looked at each other, but said nothing. They stayed huddled together in a corner of the deck, as far away from the sergeant's corpse as possible. There was no need for them to carry on pretending to be Mo's hostages and Tayeb thought about waving his gun at the policeman, but there didn't seem much point. The pig was shit-scared anyway.

As they neared Hammersmith Bridge, Mo ordered the constable to slow down. He scanned the river banks for any sign of continued surveillance and, satisfied there was none, started looking around for a suitable landing site.

He finally selected a jetty on the north bank, just beyond the western end of the Hammersmith flyover. Hopefully the police would be slow to pick up on a northeast trail to Notting Hill, and would concentrate their efforts on Hammersmith and Fulham. As soon as they touched dry land, he was going to have to kill their driver. The only question was how. Shooting the man would attract a lot of unwelcome attention in a semi-suburban neighbourhood like this.

Terrified as he was, the constable had kept some semblance of his wits about him. As they approached the jetty, he could see that his useful life was coming to an end. And that meant the knacker's yard. He had about ten seconds to conceive and execute an effective strategy for saving his own skin, without further endangering the lives of the other hostages.

'Why me?' he groaned, guiding the launch in alongside the jetty.

A light touch of reverse brought the boat to a complete stop. Mo flipped the pistol round in his hand. Holding it by the barrel, he raised it over the policeman's head.

But the constable had started moving the moment he felt the point of the gun lift from his back. He shoved the drive control to full ahead, and threw himself forwards over the wheel.

Mo stumbled back as he swiped down with the pistol butt, thrown off balance by the sudden lurch of the boat. A split second later, the constable killed the engine, whipped around and jumped at him. On pure reflex, Mo stuck out the pistol to defend himself, but he was still holding it by the barrel.

As the two men collided, the gun went off. They wrestled briefly on the deck of the launch, until the constable realised that he was the only one doing any wrestling. He pulled himself away and watched, mesmerised, as the blood soaked up through Mo's bomber jacket from the bullet wound in his chest.

Tayeb jumped up, reaching behind him for his gun. Rashida stuck her left arm between his legs and grabbed him by the balls. He sat down again with a painful gasp, clutching his groin. She clamped her right hand over his mouth and whispered urgently in his ear.

'Do you know what happened to me – where they kept me and everything?'

Tayeb nodded, his eyes watering slightly.

'Then you were with me, all the time, from my flat to where we are now, understand? Neither of us know this boy, why he held us hostage or why the others did. That's the story.'

She glanced nervously at the policeman, who was

engaged in the supremely ironic endeavour of attempting to resuscitate Mo by means of the kiss of life.

Tayeb pulled Rashida's hand away.

'One, I do know him – we've been friends for years,' he hissed. 'Two, I've got an identical pistol stuck in the back of my jeans.'

The constable decided that he had wasted enough breath on Mo. He knelt up and looked proudly at the hostages he had rescued. Rashida turned on a beautiful smile, full of warmth and gratitude.

'One, you didn't know he did things like *this*. Two, get rid of the gun,' she whispered, as she raised herself to her feet.

She skipped across the deck and flung her arms around the policeman's neck.

'Oh officer, how can we ever repay you – you've surely saved our lives,' she babbled, wondering what people said when their lives had *really* just been saved.

As Rashida strove to produce tears of hysterical relief, nearly bringing on a disastrous fit of the giggles instead, Tayeb eased the gun out from behind his back and dropped it over the side of the launch.

The constable happily returned Rashida's embrace, savouring his moment of heroism. She didn't let him go until Tayeb hobbled up and nudged her in the ribs. As she stepped back, the constable turned his attention to Tayeb for the first time.

'Are you hurt, son?' he asked, with genuine concern.

Tayeb was standing half bent over, his hands on his knees, looking very uncomfortable.

'Nah, it's nothing,' he lied manfully.

'Good lad,' murmured the constable, giving him a comforting pat on the back. 'Good lad.'

CHAPTER 24

Miss Holmes tapped lightly on Dexter's office door and went through. She was surprised to find her employer lying on the floor in front of his desk, his arms folded over his face. She coughed delicately.

'I'm sorry to disturb you, Mr Dexter, but you weren't answering your intercom.'

Dexter groaned softly and let his arms fall by his sides. He turned his head to look at his secretary. She politely averted her gaze, making use of the time to conduct a minute examination of her nails. No cracks or chips and the varnish was perfectly applied.

'What now?' asked Dexter, turning back to stare at the ceiling.

'We have a Mr Aziz in reception who wishes to see you,' Miss Holmes replied. 'He doesn't have an appointment,' she added, with a disapproving sniff.

Dexter sat up very slowly.

'I no longer have any means of getting rid of him,' he said wearily.

'I could inform the gentleman that you are presently unavailable,' Miss Holmes suggested.

Dexter shot her an impatient glance, then reached up on top of his desk and pulled himself to his feet. Aziz had been right. He was too old to fight. But then, he should be rich enough not to have to – and that might yet prove to be the case. He walked round behind the desk and sat down heavily on his chair.

'Show him in.'

'Yes, Mr Dexter.'

Miss Holmes felt quite light-headed with relief as she stepped out of the office. A moment of unsettling oddness had intruded on the working day, but now everything was back to normal. She buzzed reception to let the visitor up.

As Aziz passed by her desk, he gave her a lovely smile. She beamed back at him. It *was* nice to be appreciated – even by a coloured gentleman.

Dexter was considerably less enchanted by the sight of Aziz's grinning face. He watched sullenly as the Arab settled himself in the chair opposite. Then Aziz actually laughed.

'Why so glum, Steven?' he asked, still chuckling to himself.

Dexter winced at the impertinent use of his first name, but otherwise offered no response.

'Look at it this way,' Aziz went on. 'My daughter has been safely returned to me, the murderer of your son is dead – we should both be content. There have been a number of regrettable casualties – '

He snorted with irrepressible mirth, but soon got himself back under control.

'These casualties are a purely incidental and, I think, inevitable result of engaging in open warfare. So let us shake hands like good men, and return to business.'

Aziz held his hand out across the desk. Dexter ignored it.

'Your intelligence is incomplete,' he said drily.

'In what way – incomplete?' Aziz asked suspiciously.

'We had already identified one of the murderers, before the whole operation descended into – '

Dexter clasped his hands together and frowned irritably.

'This murderer,' he continued, 'is still very much alive, and is trying to convince the police that he was an innocent hostage of the other murderer, whom we had not previously identified. I have advised the police of his guilt, but in the absence of proof they are legally obliged to accept his protestations of innocence.'

'Since you have no proof, you can only be guessing,' Aziz surmised.

'Not at all,' Dexter retorted.

He opened the top drawer of his desk and took out a small colour photograph, which he handed to Aziz. It was a poor quality print of a print, with a large overexposed patch in the centre foreground. Off to one side was the shadowy figure of a young Arab man.

'This was passed to me as a photograph of the murderer of my son. It also happens to be a photograph of the boy who was recovered by the police with your daughter. *Ergo* the two persons in question are one and the same.'

Aziz examined the picture with renewed interest. The young man was presumably his deceased sergeant major's mysterious comrade.

'So you see,' Dexter added by way of conclusion, 'it is hard for me to be content with this state of affairs.'

Aziz slipped the photograph into his briefcase, and shrugged dismissively.

'You hope to *persuade* me to do something about it?' he sneered.

'I wish to purchase a service,' Dexter replied. 'I am offering a fee of fifty thousand pounds sterling for the death of the murderer.'

Aziz paused to reflect. He was extremely wary of being drawn into one of Dexter's carefully constructed traps.

'Why do you want *me* to do it?'

'I don't care who does it,' said Dexter. 'I am offering the

contract to you, because you are in the best position to carry it out.'

'What makes you think that?'

Dexter looked at him curiously.

'Surely you are aware that this *creature* and your daughter are lovers?'

Aziz opened his mouth to issue a denial, and shut it again without saying a word. The whole phenomenon of Mohammed and his friend was beginning to make sense at last. Now he would have to either dispose of the boy, or actively protect him from whoever else Dexter hired to do the job.

'Leave it with me,' he said finally, rising and offering his hand for a second time.

Dexter shook it firmly.

'I am already impatient for a result,' he said pointedly.

Aziz smiled reassuringly, then turned and left the office. Dexter flipped a switch on his intercom.

'Yes, Mr Dexter?'

'Clear my diary, Miss Holmes. I'm having the rest of the week off.'

'Yes, Mr Dexter.'

He thought he might take his wife for a short holiday somewhere. She had been terribly upset by David's death. The Canaries weren't too common at this time of year, and one of their friends had an apartment there.

Better still, he thought, *I'll take my mistress*.

CHAPTER 25

Rashida awoke to an insistent buzzing noise. She opened her eyes and propped herself up on one elbow. There was somebody at the door. The alarm clock told her it was only seven in the morning. The somebody had just robbed her of four hours' sleep.

Feeling completely unforgiving, she shrugged on her bathrobe and wrapped a white cotton scarf round her head. When she got to the bottom of the stairs, she croaked bad-temperedly through the front door.

'Who's there?'

'It's me,' came the answer.

'And who the hell are you?'

'It's me – Tayeb.'

Rashida drew back the two new security bolts and pulled open the door. It was Tayeb. He was holding an enormous bouquet of white, pink and red roses, but he looked like he had spent the night in a gutter.

Still, she thought, *if I look anything like I feel, I'm amazed he didn't turn to stone the moment he set eyes on me.*

'Come on up,' she said, as welcomingly as she could manage.

When they reached the top of the stairs, Tayeb presented her with the flowers.

'Thank you, they're beautiful,' she said vaguely, carrying them through to the kitchen alcove.

She made a quick grab for the percolator and packed it full of her darkest roast Jamaican coffee. Tayeb watched in silence as she put the percolator on the stove and looked out a pair of cups. The burst of energy that had got him there was fading fast. He sat down at the table and rested his head on his hands. It felt so good finally to be able to relax.

'I hardly think it's fair for you to wake me up so I can watch you sleep,' said Rashida.

Tayeb lifted his head to see her sitting opposite, smiling at him over a cup of coffee, a cigarette trailing smoke from her other hand. He rubbed his aching head and stretched his arms out behind the back of his chair. He felt crippled with exhaustion and completely disorientated.

'Where've you been?' Rashida asked gently.

'Paddington pig station,' he muttered.

He took a sip of coffee, then helped himself to one of her cigarettes.

'All this time?'

'Sevenny-two hours,' he yawned. 'They only let me go because they had to.'

'But they believed your story?'

Tayeb shrugged, then lit his cigarette.

'They couldn't prove any different,' he said finally.

Rashida felt a deep sense of relief. If the story hadn't held up, it would have been at least as much her fault as anybody else's.

'Then you're in the clear?' she asked hopefully.

'Pretty much, I guess,' Tayeb answered, smiling for the first time that morning.

She leaned in towards his smile. They kissed, long and sweet. As they drew apart, the door buzzer sounded again. A second mystery caller – and it wasn't even eight o'clock. Rashida felt the screaming tension of the past few days pile itself back on her shoulders.

'I'd better see who it is,' she said wearily.

'I'll cover you,' said Tayeb, jumping to his feet.

'What with?' she asked, glancing around the room. 'A bunch of roses?'

Tayeb took her point, but still followed her out as far as the landing. If anything happened to her, he wanted to be in a position to do something about it right away. He lay on the floor and watched through the bannisters as Rashida went down to the front door.

'Who is it?' she called.

'Your father.'

She pulled a face and waved Tayeb back into the flat. Once he was out of sight she opened the door. Aziz walked past her into the hallway, without waiting to be invited. Rashida hurriedly took up a fallback position at the foot of the stairs.

'I'm afraid you can't come up right now,' she said firmly.

Aziz looked at her sourly.

'And what secret could a daughter – especially an *unmarried* daughter – possibly keep from her father?' he wondered out loud.

She blushed in spite of herself.

'Don't worry – I know all about your little friend,' he went on. 'I am here to see him also.'

Rashida didn't like the sound of that. She hoped Tayeb realised how dangerous a man her father could be. But for now, at least, it was not in her power to protect him.

'All right,' she said brusquely, turning and leading the way up the stairs.

As Aziz entered the room, and before he had had the chance to do or say anything, Tayeb thought he had better make one thing clear.

'I didn't grass you up,' he said quickly.

'I know.'

Aziz sat down at the table, folded his arms, and looked Tayeb closely up and down. Tayeb stared straight back at him, just too plain tired to be fazed by his first interview with The Boss. Rashida watched them both from the end of her bed, already beginning to fear for Tayeb.

A moment later, to Rashida's great surprise, her father started to smile.

'Very good,' said Aziz. 'Every bit as brave as your fallen comrade.'

Tayeb didn't know how to reply, so he kept his mouth shut.

'Circumspect too – I like that,' Aziz continued, after a short pause. 'However, you have been a little careless in at least one respect.'

He put his briefcase on the table, flipped it open and pulled out a buff office folder. From this he extracted a small colour photograph, which he slid across the table to where Tayeb was standing.

'Who's that?' he asked.

Tayeb picked up the photo. He recognised the subject in the background immediately.

'It's me,' he said simply.

'I regret to say that the original is in the hands of our enemies who, I should add, have placed a flatteringly large price on your head.'

Tayeb shifted his weight uneasily from one foot to the other. An overwhelming feeling of fatigue was making it hard for him to think constructively.

Aziz allowed sufficient time for the full weight of his announcement to sink in, then went on.

'Your life is in danger for as long as you remain in London or, for that matter, any other Western city. In order to repay your loyalty, and in recognition for the considerable service you have done me, I would be happy to fully finance the continuation of your training and education in a secure region of the Arab world.'

'Where's that?' asked Tayeb.

'I have contacts in Libya, Algeria and Egypt.'

He turned to his daughter.

'And you may accompany him as his wife, if you both so wish. As you can see,' he continued, turning back to Tayeb, 'she is resolutely not mine to give. If it were otherwise, I should happily offer her to you – '

Rashida paled with righteous fury. She swept up to the table, slammed the top of her father's briefcase down and shoved it into his arms.

'Get out,' she said, through clenched teeth.

Aziz shrugged, snapped his briefcase properly shut and stood up. He addressed Tayeb one last time.

'You will let me know? Soonest would be best.'

Tayeb nodded. Aziz turned and left the room.

Rashida sat down at the table and lit another cigarette. She picked up her cup of coffee and put it down again. It was stone cold.

'What do you think?' Tayeb asked uncertainly.

'I think . . .' she began, 'I think that *you* will have to accept his offer and then *we* will never see each other again.'

Tears for fading happiness rolled down her cheeks. She tried to brush them away with the back of her hand, but too many fell too fast. Tayeb rushed to her side, wrapped his arms around her and did his best to comfort her. But it was no use.

They both knew she was right.

CHAPTER 26

It was dark by the time Tayeb sneaked out of his house to keep the appointment he had made with Aziz. Even dressed all in black, with ski cap and mirror shades, he wasn't half as invisible as he wanted to be. The large sports bag he had slung over his shoulder held his Walkman, cassette collection and as many of his clothes as he could cram into it. He wondered if everyone in Libya wore sheets, like Aziz did.

If it hadn't been for the memory of Mo's dead body, he wouldn't be going anywhere. It just lay there in his imagination, reminding him of how real the possibility of getting killed was. Maybe Tripoli would be fun – though Africa always looked like shit on TV.

Tayeb glanced around one more time to check that he wasn't being followed, then darted into the West London Development Partnership's stainless steel and smoked glass building. He was met at the reception desk by a male secretary, who greeted him pleasantly before showing him through to Aziz's office.

'Very good,' said Aziz, as the two young men entered the room.

He motioned Tayeb to a seat and talked briefly with his secretary. They spoke in Arabic. Tayeb couldn't understand a word and immediately began to feel paranoid, but Aziz quickly reverted to English.

'That is excellent news – my congratulations. We shall talk more later.'

The secretary took the hint, and withdrew.

'Hassan is to be married,' Aziz explained. 'I see that you, however, are to be on your own,' he went on. 'That is a great pity.'

Tayeb nodded. It was a *major* downer, as far as he was concerned.

'I am sorry. But maybe it will be for the best.'

'Maybe,' Tayeb echoed doubtfully. 'We couldn't just, well, hang out together?'

'Not where you're going,' Aziz said bluntly. 'Did you bring your passport?'

'Yeah.'

Tayeb handed it over. Aziz took a large rubber stamp and inkpad out of the bottom drawer of his desk. He inked up the stamp, opened Tayeb's passport at the first clean page, and carefully pressed the stamp on to it.

'That's your visa,' said Aziz. 'It will pass inspection by any customs or immigration official.'

Tayeb took the passport back and stuck it in his jacket pocket.

'Now your airline ticket,' Aziz continued. 'You will fly from Gatwick to Paris, Charles de Gaulle – where you will pick up a connecting flight to Tripoli. Your Paris flight leaves in under three hours so you should go straight to the airport as soon as we are finished here.'

Tayeb put the ticket away with his passport.

'A good friend of mine will meet you at Tripoli airport. I have something for you to give him.'

Aziz picked up a small canvas bag from behind his chair and handed it to Tayeb. The zip was fastened with a miniature combination padlock. Tayeb eyed it suspiciously.

'Don't worry,' smiled Aziz. 'It's only private documents, nothing illegal.'

'What's your friend's name?' asked Tayeb.

Aziz hesitated.

'He will approach you.'

'I don't like it,' Tayeb said frankly.

'Listen to me,' retorted Aziz. 'You will be in great danger until you reach Libya. I cannot allow you to be in possession of compromising intelligence, except insofar as is absolutely necessary. I have already taken considerable risks in assisting you this far; I am not prepared to endanger loyal friends as well.'

Tayeb thought about it. He reckoned he might have caught a faint whiff of bullshit, especially around the *Aziz taking risks* part of the speech. But he had seen enough war movies to know that the best way of not giving secrets to the enemy was not knowing any in the first place.

'OK,' he agreed finally.

'Then our business is complete – for now. Hassan!'

The door swung open. Tayeb picked up his bags and walked out of the office, escorted by the male secretary. When they reached reception, Hassan took hold of Tayeb's shoulders and kissed him on both cheeks. The deadly smell of his breath made Tayeb's nose wrinkle. Hassan laughed.

'You're so British,' he said.

'Yeah, well – I've gotta go,' Tayeb answered, pulling away.

'Of course.'

Hassan stood smiling and waving goodbye as Tayeb hurried off down the street towards the tube station. Then he went back through to Aziz's office.

'Come in, come in,' Aziz said warmly. 'Now sit down and tell me how you managed to persuade her.'

'It wasn't too difficult,' replied Hassan. 'Your daughter

is a very strong-willed but also a very intelligent woman. She understands that the qualities one looks for in a husband are not the same as those one enjoys, temporarily, in a lover.'

'How true,' chuckled Aziz. 'It goes without saying that you have my blessing. As soon as I receive word from abroad, we may celebrate the successful conclusion of both affairs.'

The Gatwick Express felt cool, fast and comfortable, but far from safe. Tayeb became convinced that the man wheeling the buffet trolley up the aisle was an enemy agent. He even *looked* Jewish. As he approached, Tayeb braced himself. Maybe some kind of poisoned dart would shoot out from the side of the trolley, and it would show up in the *post mortem* like he had died of a heart attack.

The trolleyman looked briefly in his direction, and went on by. Tayeb was relieved at first; then it occurred to him that he had probably just been fingered by the look-out man. And that meant the real assassin knew exactly where he was.

He waited until the trolley had passed through the next carriage towards the front of the train, then snatched up his bags and hurried down to the rear. He settled in next to a colourful Nigerian family, who were rowing noisily with one another in some incomprehensible language – apparently about who got to put their feet up on the suitcases.

The argument was still going strong as the train pulled into Gatwick Airport. Tayeb stuck with his adopted family as far as the check-in hall. He knew that from there on in, security was going to be pretty tight.

Within an hour, he was sitting on his plane, feeling much more relaxed. He got quite a buzz out of taking off, and it seemed like they were in the air for only a couple of minutes before he had to refasten his seatbelt and prepare for landing.

Tayeb had stuffed the little bag Aziz had given him inside his sports bag and taken it as hand luggage. With the strap biting ever deeper into his shoulder as he lumbered along endless corridors to the transit lounge, he began to wish he had checked it in. But at least this way he, his clothes and his music would all arrive in Libya together.

When he finally reached the lounge, he discovered that there was a four-hour wait before his next flight. He found an unoccupied bench of seats, put on his Walkman and stretched out, using his bag for a pillow.

Just as he was drifting nicely with the music, he felt someone tweak his nose. He looked up, then blinked. A fat woman in full purdah stood next to him. She was so completely veiled that he couldn't even see her eyes. It was like being confronted by an animated black cotton sack.

The sack extended a gloved hand and beckoned to him. He sat up, mystified. It could only be one of Aziz's agents – who else would know where to find him? Maybe there had been a last minute change of plan.

'What gives?' he asked warily.

'*Suivez-moi,*' answered the sack.

'Do what?'

'Follow, yes?'

'Who says?'

The sack leaned in towards him.

'Aziz,' whispered the woman inside.

That was all Tayeb needed to know. He grabbed his bag and stood up.

'Lead on, sister.'

He followed her on to a moving walkway, down under

the high dome of the airport building and along to passport control. The immigration official looked like he would have shot them both if it hadn't been for the bullet-proof glass over his desk. But he waved them through after only the most cursory glance at their passports.

They carried on past the unattended customs desk and on to the shuttle bus to the RER station. Once there, the sack hurried over to the booking office and came back with two tickets. They passed through the turnstiles and went down on to the platform, where they boarded a train for *Paris Ville*.

Tayeb was beginning to wonder whether he was doing the right thing, when he heard a warning tone and the automatic doors slammed shut. As they pulled away, the sack looked slowly up and down the carriage. They were alone.

'See what happens,' said the voice behind the veil. 'I leave you on your own for one evening and you go off with the first woman you meet.'

Tayeb's expression of total astonishment dissolved into a bewildered smile as Rashida threw off her headscarf and veil. She kissed him quickly on the lips, then jumped up and tugged off her long, black gown.

'I'm *sweltering*!'

Underneath, she was wearing baggy jeans over tight jeans over ski pants, four layers of tops and two jackets. She had a small, fully stuffed rucksack strapped across her stomach, which she couldn't wait to get rid of.

'That's better,' she sighed, flinging the jackets and rucksack on to the seat opposite and throwing herself into Tayeb's arms.

They hugged each other close. Tayeb wanted to know what the hell was going on, but he decided to kiss first and ask questions later.

After several minutes of mute passion, his curiosity finally got the better of him.

'Where're we going?'

'The Gare du Nord, then we're going to take a train to Brussels, then another train to Amsterdam. It should be safe for us to stay there a few days while we decide what to do next.'

'Why?' asked Tayeb, 'I mean – '

'Because I love you,' Rashida said simply.

'You know we aren't safe here.'

'You're safer in Paris than Tripoli, at least for the next few hours.'

'How's that?'

'My father hired a Libyan hit man to kill you.'

'What?!' yelled Tayeb.

'He's nice like that,' said Rashida. 'I don't think you were being followed, but they can easily find out from the airline that you got off at Paris. And they'll start checking as soon as you fail to arrive in Tripoli. That's why we have to go overland – they don't take your name on the railways.'

Tayeb's head was spinning. He tried to put his thoughts in some kind of order.

'How do you know all that?'

'Creepy Hassan told me,' Rashida explained. 'My father's personal assistant – he's been sliming after me for years. I said that if he told me what my father was planning for you, I'd marry him.'

'And he went for it?'

'Well I am the boss's daughter, you know.'

'I mean, he *believed* you – '

'Well, he knew I couldn't be serious about *you*, since I hadn't accepted the wedding-in-Libya proposal.'

Tayeb turned away and stared grumpily out of the

window. He had thought they should get married, if that was the only way of staying together. Aziz and that other arsehole must have been practically laughing in his face.

'Don't worry, my pretty one,' Rashida said soothingly. 'There'll be plenty of time to massage your ego later.'

She reached around him from behind, slipped her hands inside his shirt and started to tickle his stomach. Tayeb twitched and writhed, trying to stay moody – then finally surrendered to helpless laughter.

'OK, OK,' he said, fighting her hands away, then pulling her on to his lap. 'So we're together now, innit?'

She held his face in her hands and kissed him.

'I did regret it, though,' she said softly.

'Yeah?'

'Hassan told me that if I had married you, my father wouldn't have ordered your death. It would have been worthwhile keeping you alive, to keep me out of trouble.'

Tayeb shook his head and smiled.

'Well, you're in a whole lotta trouble now,' he said.

'So are you.'

They held each other tight as the train rushed on through the high-rise suburbs to central Paris. Tayeb felt wonderful. Rashida had come up with an excellent plan. There was just one possible snag which came to mind.

'How much money have you got?'

'About forty francs.'

'Meaning?'

'Nearly five pounds.'

'We're fucked.'

'You do still have the package my father gave you?' Rushida said suddenly.

'Yeah.'

Tayeb leaned down and dug out the padlocked canvas bag Aziz had given him.

'You don't know the combination?'

'No.'

She slid off Tayeb's lap and fetched a little make-up box from her rucksack. Inside were a pair of nail scissors, which she used to unpick the stitching along one end of the bag.

'Close your eyes,' she told him, then shook the contents out on to the seat opposite.

'You can look now.'

Tayeb opened his eyes and stared in disbelief at the pile of neatly bundled banknotes.

'The price on your head,' Rashida smiled. 'Fifty thousand pounds.'

Founded in 1986, Serpent's Tail publishes the innovative and the challenging.

If you would like to receive a catalogue of our current publications please write to:

FREEPOST
Serpent's Tail
4 Blackstock Mews
LONDON N4 2BR

(No stamp necessary if your letter is posted in the United Kingdom.)